"You Want Me To Pretend To Be Your Mistress?"

"Companion," he corrected. *For now.*

"Why me?"

"You're different."

Her eyes watched him. "So if I agree to this, you'll do what you promised to do? You'll investigate my claim?"

"Regrettably, you'll have to wait."

"Don't you trust me to keep to my word?"

"Never trust a woman with a grudge."

Was it a trick of the light or did she somehow look vulnerable? It made him wonder what fool had given her up. Then again, some men could only take so much of that deliciously smart mouth.

And some men liked to live dangerously.

Dear Reader,

Welcome to the next book in my Roth series, set around the second brother in this rich and powerful Australian dynasty. This story is about loyalties to family…between friends…and between lovers. Strong emotional ties link them all, yet it's those very ties that put love to the test.

And if anyone has been tested by love it's handsome widower Adam Roth. He knows how easy it is to love and to lose, so having Jenna Branson cross his path and insist that a member of his family cheated her brother has Adam stepping in to shield his remaining loved ones.

Jenna Branson simply wants the money owed to her brother. She certainly doesn't want to get emotionally involved with one of the Roths, but she finds herself unable to deny a growing attraction to a man who clearly has his own family's best interests at heart. Just as she does.

Being a hero or a heroine isn't just about loving each other. When you love, the urge to protect your loved ones is incredibly strong. You do all you can to help, even if it means divided loyalties. How heartbreakingly humiliating it would be, then, to discover those loyalties had been misplaced, and at a terrible price, too.

To win, one of this pair will need to lose. I hope you cheer for Jenna and Adam as they fall in love and seek a way to *both* come out winners.

Happy reading!

Maxine

MAXINE SULLIVAN

HIGH-SOCIETY SEDUCTION

Published by Silhouette Books
America's Publisher of Contemporary Romance

 **SILHOUETTE BOOKS**

ISBN-13: 978-0-373-73065-0

Recycling programs
for this product may
not exist in your area.

HIGH-SOCIETY SEDUCTION

Copyright © 2010 by Maxine Sullivan

Visit Silhouette Books at www.eHarlequin.com

Printed in U.S.A.

MAXINE SULLIVAN

The *USA TODAY* bestselling author credits her mother for her lifelong love of romance novels, so it was a natural extension for Maxine to want to write her own romances. She thinks there's nothing better than being a writer and is thrilled to be one of the few Australians to write for the Silhouette Desire line.

Maxine lives in Melbourne, Australia, but over the years has traveled to New Zealand, the U.K. and the U.S.A. In her own backyard, her husband's job ensured they saw the diversity of the countryside, from the tropics to the Outback, country towns to the cities. She is married to Geoff, who has proven his hero status many times over the years. They have two handsome sons and an assortment of much-loved, previously abandoned animals.

Maxine would love to hear from you. She can be contacted through her website at www.maxinesullivan.com.

Special thanks to fabulous Desire editor Shana Smith
for her cheerful assistance and
behind-the-scenes help over the years.

One

"And this is Jenna Branson. She's one of our up-and-coming jewelry designers."

Jenna heard her boss's words, thankful that at least she'd had time to recover from her shock. Having Adam Roth walk into the Conti corporate box at Australia's Flemington Racecourse a few minutes ago had stunned her.

Oh, God! she'd thought. Here was the middle son of Laura and Michael Roth, iconic owners of Roth's, the luxury-goods department stores. His family was Australia's aristocracy. The crème de la crème of Australian society. She'd never wanted to meet any one of them. Not after what Liam Roth had done to her brother.

She watched in silent horror now as this Roth family member lowered his tall, lean body onto the chair opposite. His gaze came straight at her across the table, homing in like she was the only person in the room. She hid a small gasp as his pair of blue eyes trapped hers for a heart-stopping moment in time.

"It's a pleasure to meet you, Jenna," he murmured, his gaze taking in her lustrous, shoulder-length brown hair, then the details of her face, before sliding down to the soft floral dress she knew looked good on her. For the first time ever, she actually wished she *didn't* look quite so feminine.

Jenna tried to smile, but she wasn't sure if she managed it. "Yes, you, too," she somehow said, hoping she sounded sincere but almost choking on the words. Why, oh, why had she given in to pressure and come here today? If only her boss, Roberto, and his charming wife, Carmen, hadn't been so insistent. She would have much preferred to spend her Saturday relaxing in her apartment.

"Have you backed any winners yet?" Adam asked in a smooth voice that was as cultured as it was deep.

She tried to settle her heart back in place. "Not so far."

He smiled the confident smile of a man who knew women. "Then perhaps your luck will change."

If he thought *he* was going to change her luck, he was in for a surprise. "Perhaps."

Just then her boss's son returned to the table and sat down next to her, almost making her shudder, giving her something else to worry about. Marco had been asking her out for months. Now he thought he'd worn her down. Nothing could be further from the truth.

"You didn't bring a date?" he said to Adam, after a short greeting.

"No. Not this time."

"That's not like you, *amico mio,*" he joked, but he slid his arm along the back of Jenna's chair as if silently staking a claim.

A note of awareness docked in Adam's eyes, sending an

odd ripple of apprehension shooting down her spine. She didn't want either man thinking she was here with Marco. Nor did she want either one thinking she was available for some sort of dalliance.

Unfortunately, as the afternoon wore on, she was fully aware of Adam surreptitiously watching her every movement. She tried her damnedest not to react, but his interest was a living thing. It made her uneasy, though not in a sleazy way like with her boss's son. Adam Roth was a playboy. A sophisticated master playboy, despite being a widower whose wife had died in a car accident over four years ago. She had no doubt he knew all the right moves.

One thing saved her. Her brother. Remembering what Stewart had been through gave her the advantage. She knew what this man's family was capable of, and that helped put up an invisible barrier to deflect any attempt at intimacy.

By the time they'd finished eating a late lunch, she was more than ready to make an escape to the powder room. Thankfully, Marco was involved in watching the next race with another woman and her generous cleavage. So while everyone was occupied Jenna grabbed her purse to slip out of the room, her heartbeat stuttering when she saw Adam notice her leaving.

Once in the corridor she hurried along the plush carpet to find the ladies' room. She had a feeling he would follow. That he was about to ask her out. She didn't want that, she decided as she found what she was looking for just ahead. She reached for the door handle...started to open it...

"Jenna."

She stilled, tempted to ignore him and go inside the room but suspected he would merely wait for her to come out. Taking a deep breath, she dropped her hand and turned around to face him.

Adam was right behind her, his proximity surprising

her, causing her knees to wobble. He reached out to cup her elbows and steady her. At his touch the sound of the race caller outside wound down to a mere whisper, and the excitement of the guests cheering their horses along the final stretch muted to low volume, making her forget everything else for a moment.

Then his eyes warmed and his firm lips spread into a sensual smile that promised to take her places she'd never been. "I think you'll find that's not what you want," he drawled, his voice a hot whisper along her spine.

She blinked. "It…isn't?"

He indicated the sign on the door. "That's a store-room."

"Oh." In her hurry, she hadn't noticed. Her mind had been focused on getting away from him. She pulled back and he dropped his hands. He was still too close.

If she'd had time to think, she would have felt foolish for rushing and making such a mistake. As it was, she half turned to take a quick look down the corridor hoping to see the ladies' room and still make her escape in the next few seconds.

But then a thought flashed through her mind. Wasn't she crazy to walk away when she had a Roth right here in front of her? Wouldn't swallowing her pride and confronting this man be a small price to pay? She'd been praying for a way to help her brother and now she had it. Heck, she had to do *something* to help Stewart.

Taking a deep breath, Jenna opened her mouth to speak, but shut it again as a young woman walked by. A hallway wasn't the place to talk about a private matter.

Instead, she gestured to the storeroom. "Do you think I could have a word alone with you?"

The oddest gleam entered his eyes. "In there?"

"Yes." She had to talk to him. Now. If she wasn't quick enough, the opportunity would pass. "Please."

Adam didn't move. He had a strange look about him. As if he were...*disappointed* in her.

He shook his head. "Sorry, beautiful. You're stunning, and I must admit I'm very tempted, but a quick grope in a broom cupboard isn't my thing. I prefer to wine and dine a woman first."

She gaped at him. "Wh-what?"

He assessed her with a touch of regret. "No doubt many a man would be pleased to make you their own on such short acquaintance, but I find a little romance is more... satisfying." He went to turn back to the function rooms. "I was going to ask you out, but—"

She pulled herself together in time to grab his arm. "You think I'm after *sex?*" she hissed, totally insulted. "I can assure you that's the last thing on my mind."

His gaze darted down to her hand on his sleeve, then up again but she refused to let go in spite of feeling the muscle beneath her palm.

"I really do need to speak to you. I prefer we do it in private...." She swallowed, then dared to threaten, "But I can do it just as well in front of an audience."

A cool look entered his eyes. "Seeing how we only met a few hours ago, I can't imagine you'd have anything of importance to say to me."

She continued her grip on his arm. "Then you'd be wrong."

There was a measured silence. "Did you engineer this meeting today?"

"No. But that doesn't mean I don't have a valid complaint about your family."

"My family?" he said, stiffening.

"Perhaps you'll let me explain in private."

There was a pause. He inclined his head. "Very well."

At his reluctant acquiescence, she finally dropped her hand, letting out a silent sigh of relief, but aware this was only the first step.

Adam reached past her and pushed open the door, indicating she should precede him into the room. He was all business now, making it clear he had nothing else on his mind. Once inside he closed the door and positioned himself in front of it. "Okay, talk."

She realized her mistake in not getting him go first into the room. She had no escape now, only a large frosted window that gave a false impression of freedom—and a short distance between her and her inadvertent captor. Oh, God, what on earth was she doing?

Then she made herself remember her brother's anguish. And that gave her the courage to press onward. She drew back her shoulders. "I want you to give my brother the money your brother Liam conned out of him."

He froze, then, "Rewind that and play it again. Slowly this time."

Oh, this man was good at keeping his cool—very good—but he'd probably had plenty of experience covering up for his late brother. Many times he would have had to lie to the people Liam Roth had duped over the years.

"I expected you to deny it. The Roths stick together." Stewart had told her that and she had no reason *not* to believe him. The rich and privileged always seemed to get away with everything. Her ex-boyfriend, Lewis, had been the same, though he was nowhere near equal to the Roths. He'd thought his money had entitled him to do whatever he liked—including cheating on her.

Adam Roth's eyes flickered with annoyance. "I can't deny something if I don't know the details," he said curtly, bringing her back to the present. His brows jerked together. "Who's your brother anyway?"

"Stewart Branson."

His expression gave nothing away. "Am I supposed to know him?" He didn't give her time to answer. "I'm afraid you're talking to the wrong guy, sweetheart. My family has nothing to do with this."

She was annoyed by his instant dismissal. "I know what my brother told me."

His jaw set. "I'd like to hear exactly what he said."

Jenna let out a slow breath, relieved he was at least willing to keep listening. "Six weeks ago there was a segment on the news about your parents attending an Australia Day dinner. They showed footage from Liam's funeral." Adam's younger brother had died from a terminal illness in early December.

He didn't move. "Go on."

"Stewart had dropped by my apartment. He looked terrible. I was just about to ask him what was wrong when he looked at the television and saw the funeral procession and broke down. He said your brother had tricked him into giving him a large sum of money he could ill afford." She could still remember how appalled she'd been at what she'd learned.

"Liam wouldn't do that."

"I'm afraid he did," she said with total conviction.

"He had his own money. He didn't need anyone else's."

She tilted her head. "Didn't he invest in a failed theme park up north?" It had been in all the papers recently. She even remembered Liam's name in particular because of his death.

Now, *that* appeared to get Adam Roth's attention.

"Go on."

The air was tight with tension, but Jenna couldn't let trepidation get to her. "Around two years ago Stewart met Liam at a function and—"

"What function?" Adam fired at her.

She tried to think, but it was hard with him staring her down like this. "I don't know. Stewart didn't say."

Adam's brows drew together, then he murmured, "That's around the time my brother found out he was sick."

"I know," she said quietly, feeling bad for bringing all this up again. "But that doesn't change anything. Your brother still took the money."

His mouth flattened. "I'm not convinced."

Jenna hated this. As far as she was concerned she shouldn't have to convince him of anything. It just *was*.

"I believe they discussed the theme park venture and Liam assured him it would be no risk. Foolishly, Stewart used his house as collateral and gave him three hundred thousand dollars."

Adam gave a harsh laugh. "Three hundred thousand? And he handed it over without question?"

"Stewart trusted your brother," she said, her teeth setting on edge. "I mean, he's a Roth, right? Your family's integrity is supposed to be beyond question."

"It *is* beyond question." His whole demeanor said she'd offended him.

"So where's my brother's money then? They were supposed to start building the theme park six months ago, only there were delays on top of delays. Finally the company went bust, as you would know." It was in the media. No one could have missed it, nor the fact that Liam had been one of the investors, notwithstanding being terminally ill at the time. "My brother believes that Liam took the money under false pretenses, and so do I. Your family owes it to Stewart to repay the full amount."

His gaze sliced over her. "Where's your brother now?"

"He's an architect. He's gone off to the Middle East to try and earn some fast money so he won't lose his family home. Fortunately, he's managed to keep up his house payments until recently, but now…" Her heart constricted with pain. "*And* he's got a wife and two small children who are missing him badly. They want him home, but he won't return until he has enough to keep the bank happy and to stop him from losing the house."

The worst thing for Jenna was not being able to talk to anyone about this. She'd been keeping it all to herself. Both her parents and Stewart's wife thought he'd simply gone overseas to pay off his house sooner. Poor Vicki had no idea she was at risk of losing their gorgeous family home of which she was so proud.

"Why didn't he come to me himself?" Adam asked. "Surely you shouldn't have to do your brother's dirty work for him?"

She didn't appreciate his tone. "Stewart said it was no use talking to your family about it because you'd close ranks anyway." She studied his hostility. "I see what he means." Stewart had been a total mess that day at her place, and she wouldn't have him worrying over her involvement in this now. She'd get it sorted first.

He fixed her with an intense stare. "There's a legal system in place to protect him. Has he started proceedings?"

"How can he do that? He doesn't have the money. And besides, he had to find a way to stop his wife and children from being thrown out on the street *now*. Once he gets that sorted, you can bet he'll be back to take you to court." Her lips twisted. "Not that it would do him much good. No doubt your legal team will find a way to evade paying up in the end."

A muscle ticked in his cheekbone. "I don't take kindly to insults to my family."

"That's a shame," she mocked, then felt a twinge of conscience. Usually she didn't have a nasty bone in her body, but after what this man's late brother had done to Stewart, she knew she couldn't back down.

"What do you want me to do about it?"

She steeled herself. "Give him his money so he can come back and be with his family."

"I'm expected to hand over three hundred thousand dollars on the word of you and your brother?" He gave a terse laugh.

"It would save a lot of trouble…and embarrassment for your family."

He shot her a chilled look. "Don't try and blackmail me, Ms. Branson."

He could be as formal as he liked, but it didn't change anything. "It's not blackmail. It's a promise."

She'd never suspected she would have the heart, but if she had to, she would find a way to take this to his parents or to his older brother, Dominic, who'd recently married Liam's widow, Cassandra. She prayed she didn't have to. Yet thinking about it, she knew Adam was definitely the one most approachable over such a matter, regardless of the ice-cold look he was giving her at this precise moment.

"If you do anything to upset my parents," he warned, sending a shiver under her skin that had nothing to do with the coolness of the room, "I'll make you pay and pay dearly."

She held her ground. "Then why not *pay* my brother back his money and save everyone the hassle?"

"I don't do business that way."

"Obviously."

He watched her in silence, then his look turned as sleek

as silk. "I see Roberto and Carmen think highly of you." His tone was idle, but she knew better.

"Yes." All at once she could feel her control of the situation slipping away, but had no idea how to get out of it.

"And Marco wants you."

"That's not my problem."

"I see." He offered her a sudden, satisfied smile that didn't reach his eyes. "I wonder if Roberto would be interested in knowing one of his employees is taking advantage of his hospitality today for her own purposes?"

She glared at him. "*Now* who's blackmailing whom?"

His shoulders rose and fell. "I'm just saying that if I let it be known I'm not happy, then you'll lose your job. I doubt you'll get another one with such a prestigious company."

A lump wedged in her throat. "I get your point, but it doesn't change a thing. If you don't do right by my brother, *I* won't do right by you and your family."

A hint of admiration entered his eyes. "I like your style. You don't back down much."

She angled her chin at him. "I'd like to think I don't back down at all."

His lips twitched, then he sobered. "I need time to investigate this claim of yours to see if it's bogus or not."

"It's not bogus."

"Then humor me and let me go through the motions." He considered her with slow deliberation, and something stirred inside her. "In the meantime you could do me a favor."

She stiffened. "*Me* do *you* a favor? I don't see how I could do that, and I don't see why I should anyway."

"Let me finish," he chided, a warning light in his eyes. "I need a...female companion."

She looked at him in utter disbelief. "You want me to

become your *mistress?*" She'd heard of things like this happening, but—

"No, I want you to be my companion for a few weeks."

The thought still staggered her. "No, absolutely not."

"No?"

"I won't do it. I'd rather go to the media and let them sort you out."

"Don't forget there are always two sides to every story, Jenna. I have family I love and so do you, apparently. We don't want to see them hurt any more than they have been." He assessed her with narrowing eyes. "Do we?"

She released a shaky breath. "No, we don't."

"Then let's make a truce," he said, looking pleased by her answer. "I'll look into the situation about the money, but you've got to promise me a few weeks of your time."

She blinked. "Why me?"

"That's a fair question…." They heard voices outside in the corridor as people walked past. "But not one I want to talk about right now. Are you free for dinner this evening?"

"I suppose so," she said, but her stomach was dipping as if she was on a roller coaster.

"What a refreshing attitude."

"Get used to it."

He ignored that as he handed her a business card. "Call that number on the back and give them your address. A driver will pick you up at eight and bring you to my apartment."

"I have my own car. And I'd prefer to go to a restaurant if you don't mind."

"And I'd prefer to talk in the privacy of my own home." He reached for the door handle. "My driver's available. Use him." Then, giving her one last look, he left the storeroom, closing the door behind him again.

She stood there for a few minutes, catching her breath and thinking over what had just occurred. Somehow he'd turned the tables on her and now she had to consider his ludicrous proposition. His companion for a couple of weeks? He said it wasn't as his mistress, but was she being naive? Surely he knew other women who would be better suited to such a task. Some would probably even see sex as a free perk.

Why her?

Truth be told, she was intrigued and a little flattered, but she still didn't intend to take him up on such an outrageous offer. She'd go to dinner if that's what he wanted. She'd even listen to what he had to say, if it was the only way she would see any of Stewart's money, but that was all she'd do.

Looking down at the card in her hand, she realized too late she'd have to use his car service tonight after all. He hadn't given her his address and she wouldn't be able to get there otherwise. It galled her that he'd think she would easily do his bidding, but needs must.

Her resolve firmly in place, she left the storeroom and took a few steps to go back to the corporate box, but decided she couldn't face any of them a moment more this afternoon. She already had her purse, so she left a message at the hospitality desk thanking her hosts but telling them she had a headache and it was best she go home. Her boss and his wife should understand, and she doubted Marco would even realize she'd gone.

Something told her that Adam Roth wouldn't be so forgiving in his place.

Two

Adam finished dressing, then glanced at his gold watch as he slipped it back on his wrist. Seven-thirty. Jenna Branson would be here soon.

She hadn't come back to the corporate box after their discussion in the storeroom, yet he knew she had gumption, that one. Beautiful and a sexy challenge, he would enjoy spending the next month with her, but it had been her unrelenting attitude this afternoon that had him conceiving an idea to sort out a major hassle in his life. With his best friend's wife showing clear signs of having "the hots" for him, he was becoming increasingly concerned. How long before Chelsea gave herself away in front of Todd? He couldn't let that happen, not for his friend's sake, nor his own.

Right now he needed someone like Jenna. Someone who could stand up for herself, but not get emotionally involved. Someone who at the end of the month would leave without having to be asked. Oh, yeah, she would definitely be happy to walk away from him. She was so unlike some of the women he knew, who preferred to simper and do his bidding at the click of his fingers and were more a pain in the butt than not.

Of course, not all the women he knew were like that. There were some he admired, like his sister-in-law Cassandra, who reminded him very much of his mother. Both women had the same sense of compassion and integrity, yet fought for what they believed in. Both women put their family first. He liked that in a person whether they were male or female.

Family was family.

And keep your enemies close, he reminded himself, as he left his bedroom and went into the open-plan living room. Jenna Branson was the enemy, when all was said and done. She could cause immense anguish for his parents if she pursued the avenue that Liam had conned her brother out of a large sum of money.

The problem was that he *wasn't* sure Liam hadn't done such a thing. He missed his younger brother terribly, and heaven knew Liam hadn't deserved to die so young, but if anyone had gone through life taking what he wanted, it had been Liam.

That wasn't to say his brother would have conned this Stewart Branson out of his money. Liam hadn't been a con man. But he *had* tried to get others to invest money in the theme park, unable to see it hadn't been a good investment. Along with Dominic, Adam had tried to convince their brother not to go ahead with it. It had been just before the diagnosis of his illness, but as far as he knew, Liam had still invested in the theme park, though thankfully it had only been a quarter of a million dollars, not the half a million he'd originally planned on.

And all that left a question unanswered, settling a hard knot in his stomach. Who was to say Liam hadn't convinced Jenna's brother to invest money, as well? And the fool may well have gone and done it. Until *he* discovered the truth he wouldn't rest.

Jenna Branson needn't know that.

Just then the concierge phoned to say Jenna was on her way up to the penthouse, and Adam felt a kick of excitement as he went to meet her at the private elevator. Curbing his desire while keeping her close was certainly going to be a challenge. One he would enjoy.

The elevator doors slid open with a soft ping and inside stood a stunningly lovely woman in a black dress, her long legs tapering down to high-heeled shoes. With her hair back in a chignon and her exquisitely smooth features, she was even lovelier than he remembered. He made a decision then. He didn't need to pressure any woman into being his mistress, but if this willowy brunette wanted more, he wouldn't say no.

"You obviously had enough time to make yourself beautiful," he murmured, as she stepped onto the plush carpet inside his apartment.

The hint of a blush enchanted him as she came closer.

She gave a thin smile. "You should save the compliments for the real women in your life, Adam."

"You're not real?" He liked the sound of his name on her lips.

She stopped a few feet away. "I'm your worst nightmare."

Laughter escaped from him. "No woman's ever told me that before."

"Just goes to show there's always a first time."

He let his amusement slide, then paused deliberately. "I've got to agree there. The first time is *always* special."

Something wavered in her eyes before she stepped past him. He caught the captivating scent of her perfume as she moved. Midnight Poison, if he wasn't mistaken. Its seductiveness...its name...suited her.

"Nice place you have here," she said a few moments later, glancing around the luxurious surroundings, giving him glimpses of her back view that were equally as eye-catching as her front. "Very tasteful." She turned and shot him a wry look. "I'm surprised though. I thought you'd at least have an *Arabian Nights* theme. For your harem, that is."

He chuckled. "This is my nonharem apartment." He saw her lips curve up at the corners. "Good. You can smile."

Her smile instantly disappeared. "Don't get used to it. I usually only smile for the people I like."

"Then you must like me," he mocked, enjoying verbally fencing with this woman. *Really* enjoying it. She was a breath of fresh air.

Her mouth quirked some more but she turned away and placed her purse on the coffee table. When she looked back, she was serious again. "Shall we get down to business?"

"Let's have a drink before dinner." He headed for the bar. "White wine okay?" he said over his shoulder.

There was a tiny silence. "Um...yes, thank you."

He could feel her eyes on him. He knew the effect he had on women, but this woman's mixture of coolness and reluctant responsiveness wasn't something he'd previously encountered. He was intrigued.

Carrying two flutes of wine toward her, he handed her one. "Come outside and look at the view."

"I've seen it before."

He cupped her elbow with his free hand, her skin soft beneath his palm. "Not from my balcony you haven't."

On the balcony he pointed out places of interest. "There's

the Royal Botanic Gardens over there," he said, moving closer, feeling her inch away, oddly pleased by her reaction. "And the Dandenong Ranges way over there." He moved closer again.

"Stop testing me, Adam."

She was astute, this one. "Is that what I was doing?"

"You know very well you are. And I don't appreciate it," she said, a pulse hammering at the base of her throat. Yet she didn't move away. Jenna stood her ground and he realized she meant it. He sensed there was a part of her that wanted him, but she wasn't going to take it further. It was a new experience for him. Not even Maddie had—

The old pain kicked in. Maddie was long gone. Nearly five years in fact. Their child would have been four, if their unborn baby hadn't died along with its mother.

He shoved aside his thoughts. His world had moved on. "Let's eat," he rasped, twisting on his heels and going back inside the apartment, putting one foot in front of the other like he always did when the grief got to him. He heard her follow him, but he concentrated on going into the kitchen, getting the first course that his housekeeper had left in the refrigerator.

By the time he carried two plates of chicken and mango salad into the dining area, he was back in total control. Soon he was sitting opposite her at the table while they enjoyed their meal. Well, *he* was enjoying it. She was picking.

"You don't like the food?"

"It's fine." She cast him a candid look. "I just don't like being here, that's all."

Adam felt a flash of irritation. Her reluctance was beginning to wear a little thin. Women usually clambered over each other to get an invitation to his apartment.

And into his bed.

He took a sip of wine. "Tell me about your family."

Her eyes flashed at him as she put down her fork. "I'd prefer you tell me why you want me to be your...companion for a month. That *is* why you asked me here tonight."

"It might help me get a clearer picture of your brother," he pointed out, used to setting the pace.

She pressed her lips together, but relented. "My parents are alive and well and have just retired. Then there's Stewart and me. Stewart's older by five years. He and his wife, Vicki, have two little girls."

As always, he had to ignore a squeezing of inner pain at the mention of someone else's children. "How old are they?"

"Five and three." She gave him a cutting stare. "Old enough to miss their father."

"I don't doubt it." He wondered if Stewart missed his kids as much as they missed him. Did the man know how lucky he was to even have them? *He* sure as hell wouldn't be leaving his own kids for months on end.

Not that he planned on having any.

Not now.

The only child in his life was his year-old niece, Nicole, whom they'd recently learned was Dominic's child through artificial insemination, and not Liam's. She was a cute little thing who adored her father, and the feeling was reciprocated. It would cut out Dominic's heart to leave her for any length of time.

And that was the reason Dominic and Cassandra had taken Nicole with them on an extended honeymoon to the family vacation home in the tropics in Far North Queensland. It was the reason *he* was now officially staying here in Melbourne to help his father run Roths, instead of traveling around the country checking on their department stores and sorting out any problems, like he usually did. He had to admit it actually felt good to stay in one place this time. Before he'd felt restless and needed to move around, but lately it hadn't seemed to be enough.

The telephone rang from across the room, jerking him from his thoughts. He didn't move. Whoever it was could call back, and if it was who he thought it would be, then she'd definitely call back.

"Aren't you going to answer it?"

"No."

It gave another ring.

Jenna looked at the phone, then at him. "Don't let me stop you."

"I won't." He couldn't help but be abrupt. He was sick to death of these phone calls. He shouldn't have to put up with it. If it wasn't for—

Just then the answering machine clicked on and a husky female voice came over the line. "Adam, this is Chelsea." There was a pause. "I'm looking for Todd and I thought he might be with you. If you could phone me back when you get in, that would be great." Another pause. "I'll be waiting," she said, almost breathlessly, then hung up.

Silence settled over the room, then Jenna arched a brow. "You didn't want to talk to her?"

"*She's* the reason I need a companion."

She tilted her head at him. "I don't understand."

Right. It was time to tell her why he needed her help. He didn't like giving a stranger information that could ruin his friendship with his best friend, but on the other hand, Chelsea was trying to ruin it anyway. He had nothing to lose. Besides, if Jenna tried to use this against him, he'd destroy her and her family. No question.

He put down his fork and leaned back in his chair. "Chelsea's married to my best friend. Todd and I have known each other since we were kids. I was best man at

his wedding last year and he was my best man when I…
got married."

"You're a widower, aren't you?"

So she knew about that. Then he grimaced inwardly. He
supposed it would be hard *not* to know it. Nothing about
his family stayed out of the media long.

"Yes. I'm a widower." He hated that term. Loathed it,
in fact. It made him sound like a damn victim. He wasn't.
He'd suffered a loss. A massive one, but he'd picked himself
up. He'd moved on.

"So, what's the problem with this Chelsea?"

He renewed his focus on the present. "Think about it.
You didn't hear anything…*personal*…in her voice just
now?"

"Of course I did. She wants you."

He grimaced. Jenna made it sound like this was an
everyday occurrence. "And she's doing everything in her
power to try and get me into bed."

She seemed to pause, then sent him an intent look. "How
long has this been going on?"

"Nothing's *going on,*" he snapped. "Not on my part
anyway."

She waved a dismissive hand. "On her part then."

Dammit, Chelsea was beginning to drive him to distraction. And not in a pleasurable way, either.

"I didn't notice anything unusual until about six
weeks ago when she suddenly started coming on to me.
I did nothing to encourage her. I'm still doing nothing
to encourage her, but it doesn't seem to be helping." He
expelled a long breath. "Trouble is I really liked her before
that, too. I thought she was good for Todd."

"She's attractive?"

"Yeah, she's attractive but she's my best friend's *wife,*

Jenna. I certainly don't find the prospect of cheating on my friend to be desirable, either."

A curious look passed over her face. "I'm surprised. I thought—" She broke it off there.

"What? That I'm the type of man to break up a marriage?" His lips twisted. "Thanks very much," he said in disgust.

"You *do* have a reputation for being a playboy."

"With single women. I stay away from the married ones. That's my policy."

"Good policy," she said, and he wasn't sure if she was being sarcastic or not. "But Chelsea might not know that."

"She should," he snapped. "I've made it more than clear that I only date single women."

"You may *think* you have but—"

He scowled. "Whose side are you on anyway?"

She set her chin in a defiant line. "No one's. Not this Chelsea's and certainly not yours."

Tension gripped his shoulders, but he forcibly made them relax. "Okay, that's obvious. But getting back to the point, Chelsea hasn't come right out and said anything to me yet but she's definitely on the prowl. I need to stop this before it goes much further. I don't want her doing something she'll regret."

She acknowledged his words with a dip of her head. "Does Todd know any of this?"

"Hell, no. It would rip him apart. He really does love his wife. If I tell him what I suspect she's up to, she'll just deny it and then I'll be the one who loses a damn good friend."

She appeared to soak that up. Then her eyes narrowed. "So you want me to pretend to be your mistress for a few weeks?"

"Companion," he corrected. *For now.* "And make it a month."

Her eyes widened. "A month?" She immediately shook her head. "No way. Besides, being your companion won't work. No woman in her right mind would have a platonic relationship with *you*. Chelsea knows that. She'll suspect something's amiss."

"Fine, you can be my pretend mistress then," he said, pleased whatever way she called it. "If she thinks I'm involved with you, she might back off."

"And if she doesn't?" Jenna challenged.

"Either way, I lose." And that wasn't something he was familiar with. "If she continues to make a pest of herself, then Todd is going to realize it sooner or later, and part of him is going to blame me even if he knows I had nothing to do with it. I don't want it to get to that stage." Todd was the only one to eventually get through to him after Maddie's death. "He helped me a great deal when I needed him. I wouldn't repay him by doing the dirty on him and sleeping with his wife."

Their eyes met but Adam didn't look away. He wasn't one to talk about it, but he wasn't ashamed of needing his friend, either. Not after losing a loved one. *Two* loved ones, he thought, including the loss of his unborn child.

Jenna picked up her glass, took a sip of wine, then her gaze settled on him. "I'll ask the question I asked this afternoon at the races. Why me?"

He'd be disappointed in her if she hadn't asked the question again. "You're different. There's no emotional involvement between us." She went to speak and he held up his hand. "Except maybe dislike on your part," he mocked.

"True."

He gave a thin smile. "And at the end of four weeks, we don't have to worry about seeing each other again."

"And you don't have to worry about running into me," she mused, half to herself.

"There is that," he conceded.

Her eyes watched him, a hopeful light in them she was trying not to show, unsuccessfully. "So if I agree to this, you'll do what you promised to do? You'll investigate my claim?"

He leaned back in his chair and nodded. "Just as soon as we make an appearance together at the Mayoral Ball next Friday night. The month starts from then."

Her eyes went wide. "But today's only Saturday. That's a whole week away."

"Disappointed?"

She made a derisive sound. "Only because I want to get started straight away."

He shrugged. "Regrettably, you'll have to wait. I'm flying to Sydney tomorrow for a three-day conference, and I won't be back until Thursday morning." This was one conference he had to attend to keep on top of things with their competitors. His father would hold down the fort here, though his parents needed to go to Brisbane Thursday afternoon, leaving *him* to represent the family at the ball on Friday night.

"So you won't start the investigation before then?" she asked matter-of-factly, but he knew otherwise. "Don't you trust me to keep to my word?"

"Never trust a woman with a grudge."

"I've found you should never trust a man. Period."

He lifted one brow. "Someone I know?"

Her eyes took on a wary look. "I doubt it."

Was it a trick of the light or did she somehow look vulnerable? It made him wonder what fool had given her up. Then again, some men could only take so much of that deliciously smart mouth.

And some men liked to live dangerously.

Three

Jenna spent the next few days wondering what she'd gotten herself into by agreeing to be Adam Roth's pretend mistress. She didn't know how she was going to do this. It would mean spending a small amount of time in private with him, and a whole lot of time in public. Standing close. Touching him. Smiling. Acting like she was enamored with him.

Fat chance!

Dammit, there was already something between them that she didn't want to recognize. An awareness of each other that greatly disturbed her peace of mind. It distracted her when all she wanted to do was focus on the very reason they were together.

He'd just better keep to his end of the bargain or he was in for a big shock. He would deserve everything he got after that. She would take this to the media if necessary. She prayed she didn't have to. She didn't like being the bad guy in this, not when that title belonged to the late Liam Roth.

Yet her curiosity was piqued by all this with Chelsea and Todd. Adam had to be stuck between a rock and a hard place or he wouldn't have confided in her. He wouldn't risk her knowing such a thing. That at least gave her the confidence to believe he would do as he said.

Actually, she was amazed he had any scruples at all, and especially when it came to his best friend's wife. No doubt it was the *only* scruple he had, she mused, then decided that wasn't quite fair of her. He clearly loved his family. She could even understand him protecting his dead brother and the family name. She just didn't like that it was at *her* family's expense.

Of course there *was* one man she knew who definitely had no scruples at all, and she faced him at work on Monday morning, after apologizing to his father for her abrupt departure at the races. Roberto had been fine about it, but she had a hard time convincing Marco Conti that she'd left because of a headache and not because she'd seen him chatting up another woman and had been jealous. The man's ego was colossal, making it difficult to refuse his invitation to go to dinner with him the following Friday night. In the end, she had to tell him she already had another engagement, and for those few minutes she was thankful that was true. It was the only time she wanted to thank Adam Roth for anything.

And then Friday evening arrived and it was seven o'clock and her apartment doorbell was ringing. She hurried to check through the peephole before answering it, thinking it was Adam's driver come to escort her down to the car.

It wasn't.

It was Adam himself.

Her heart picked up pace as she patted her chignon, then

smoothed her hands down her evening dress and checked herself in the hall mirror. It would be her little secret that she'd found this dress tucked away in a secondhand store. She hadn't the money to buy a fancy new dress, not after what she'd spent on a dress for the races. And the two evening gowns she owned from when she dated Lewis weren't suitable, either. One was more for winter and the other had a wine stain on the bodice the dry cleaner hadn't been able to remove. Thankfully, dry-cleaning this secondhand dress had really brought out its depth of color.

Taking a deep breath, Jenna opened the door. She hadn't seen Adam since last Saturday night, and in his black tuxedo he looked superb and even more attractive than she remembered, if that were possible. Pictures in the newspaper hadn't done him justice, and neither had the color ones in magazines. In the flesh, the man had a serious case of handsome.

Then she realized he was standing there, his masculine appreciation spilling over her in the off-the-shoulder chiffon gown the color of deep blue sapphires. She knew she looked nice and she was pleased with that, but her aim had been to hold her head high next to Chelsea, not to draw this man's attention to herself.

Unsettled, she swung away to the living room. "I'll get my purse," she said, hoping her voice sounded even. She didn't invite him inside. She would only be a moment.

"Well, that's another first," he drawled as he followed her into the apartment and closed the door.

"What's that?" Heart thumping, she continued over to the coffee table.

"You didn't allow me to compliment you on your appearance."

She picked up her clutch purse, feigning indifference. "Was I supposed to?"

"Most women do."

"I'm not most women."

"I'm beginning to believe you're right." He paused. "But let me compliment you anyway," he murmured, his eyes darkening. "You really do look lovely tonight."

Her cheeks grew warm, but she had to remember he wasn't being nice out of the kindness of his heart. He had a motive for everything he did. "Thank you." She stepped toward him, feeling the need to get out of the apartment before—

"Did you design that necklace?"

The question stopped her in front of him, her hand going to the jewelry at her throat. "Yes. It's one of my own."

He nodded. "You'll definitely be a hit with Chelsea then. She loves jewelry."

"I'm so pleased we'll have something in common," she mocked. "Apart from you, that is."

He didn't smile.

His eyes said come closer.

Without warning Adam slipped his arm around her waist and brought her up against him, those eyes filling with purpose. "Here's one thing she *won't* have in common with you," he murmured, and brought his head down to hers.

Shock tingled through her veins and she opened her mouth, thinking to speak, but his tongue took advantage of the moment and silkily plunged inside. Her breath caught, then looped around her throat, but she couldn't seem to break free. His tongue savored the softness, the hollows, skillfully sapping her of strength until she felt like a swizzle stick swirling round and round, until she had to reach out and cling to him to stop from sinking to the ground.

He broke off the kiss and slowly peeled back. "We

needed to look like lovers," he said, his voice husky but in control.

Reality kicked in. It was clear he had enjoyed the kiss, but it hadn't shaken him up like it had her. God, his kiss had relegated every other kiss she'd ever had to the back of her mind, but he didn't need to know that. He might suspect it, but she'd never admit it. She had her pride.

Gathering herself, she quickly moved back out of reach. "You didn't need to kiss me for that. There's no one around."

"Didn't I?"

Another of his little tests, she realized, aware this really was more about him taking what he wanted than him wanting to give the impression they were lovers. Needless to say though, the hint of red lipstick at one corner of his mouth wouldn't go astray, she decided cynically, tempted to rub it off with her finger, but she didn't dare.

She raised her chin. "You're a good kisser, I'll grant you that," she said, trying to come across as worldly-wise and experienced, while totally ignoring her complete and utter meltdown in his arms.

"I'm glad you think so," he said smoothly, looking confident, arrogant and very self-satisfied.

Oh, he knew all right.

"No doubt you've had plenty of practice."

"I aim to please."

"How nice," she said sweetly, taking a step around him.

He moved in front of her, forcing her to stop. "What about you, Jenna?"

"Me?" Was he asking if she aimed to please? Please who? *Him?*

"Have you had plenty of practice kissing a man?" he

asked, clarifying, though she wasn't sure which question was more dangerous.

"That's *my* business." Suddenly the slight sting of her ex-boyfriend's comment about her "lacking" in some areas came to mind. "Why are you asking? Wasn't I any good?" she said without thinking, then could have kicked herself for giving anything away.

His eyes held a gleam of speculation. "You were superb," he assured her.

A shade of relief washed over her. Not for his sake, but for hers. "Good. I'd hate to think you were disappointed in my performance."

He considered her, and this time the gleam was a definite curiosity. "Why? Has someone been disappointed in your... performance before?"

She stiffened. "That's a very personal question."

His gaze intensified, then as if it didn't really matter, he shrugged. "Forget it." He looked at his watch. "We'd better get going," he said, all businesslike now, but she was sure he saw more than he was letting on.

All at once she felt like she was up against Goliath in the sexual stakes. She brushed past him toward the door, needing to get out of the apartment, where a sort of magnetic energy appeared to be bouncing off the walls. No, make that *magnetism*. The word summed up Adam Roth to perfection.

In the back of the limousine, Adam apologized before answering a call on his cell phone, saying it was important. Jenna didn't mind. She was merely grateful they didn't need to talk. That kiss back there had turned her upside down and she was still stunned by her reaction to a man she'd only recently met. It had been an excuse to create a sense of intimacy, but it had worked too well.

Trying to put it from her mind, she stared through the

side window and blocked out Adam's voice. She wasn't thrilled about being here, but at least her family was delighted, she mused. Telling them about her date tonight hadn't been something she'd wanted to do, but she'd had to preempt them seeing her picture in the papers with Adam over the next month. That meant earlier in the week she'd told her parents and her sister-in-law how he'd asked her to the Mayoral Ball, deciding she would field any future questions about him only as required. Unfortunately she couldn't do anything about them getting their hopes up over what was merely a smoke screen.

She'd had a very specific reason for telling them, of course. Stewart would have a heart attack if he suspected what she was doing on his behalf, so she'd asked them not to mention anything to her brother about Adam, asking them to keep it all low-key in general. She'd pointed out that Stewart was protective of her and how he'd worry if he knew she was dating another playboy. Her brother had certainly been vocal enough about her involvement with Lewis, and it hadn't been too hard for them to believe this would upset him.

Adam ended the call just as they arrived. He apologized again, this time with a charming smile that in the confines of the car pronounced his magnetism even more.

Jenna searched for something to say. "Are your parents going to be here tonight?"

"No, I'm attending on their behalf. They had a previous commitment."

"I suppose one Mayoral Ball is the same as another," she said unthinkingly.

"It does get a bit like that," he agreed, with a ghost of a smile. Then a worried look entered his eyes. "Regrettably my uncle needed to go for some medical tests. My parents thought their time better spent in Brisbane supporting him."

She winced at her own prejudgment. "That's very good of them."

"He's family," was all Adam said as the limousine glided to a stop near the Town Hall.

Luckily the Lord Mayor and Lady Mayoress's arrival ahead of them had the small media contingent focusing there, and Jenna was pleased when she and Adam were able to blend in with others and make their way inside the building without anyone taking notice.

The Melbourne Town Hall was a magnificent building well over a hundred years old, and it had taken her breath away the few times she'd been here. Every inch of it was regal and majestic, from the grandeur of the main staircase, marble foyer and glorious stained-glass windows, to the soaring ceilings crowned with chandeliers. The centerpiece of the building was the richly carved wood pipe organ that was the largest in the southern hemisphere.

The Main Hall had been decorated magnificently for the glittering event tonight, so it didn't matter that there was a slight delay in being shown to their table. But as she and Adam were being guided to the front of the room shortly after, Jenna could have groaned when she saw where they were sitting. She hadn't given it any thought before now.

"You okay?" Adam murmured in her ear.

"I didn't expect to be sitting with the Lord Mayor of Melbourne and the Lady Mayoress," she hissed.

"Don't be nervous."

"I'm sorry, but I'm not used to attending such a posh affair."

He gave a crooked smile. "They might look posh on the outside, but believe me, on the inside they're just like you and me."

"I doubt that," she muttered, then somehow managed a smile for the guests ahead.

Introductions were made to the dignitaries, though there were still a couple of vacant chairs. They were probably reserved for the Prime Minister, she thought with wry cynicism. So much for keeping a low profile. She wasn't used to quite such exalted company. For all Lewis's connections, his family would barely reach the coattails of these people.

As drinks were served, Adam leaned in close under cover of the conversation. "If it makes you feel better, just think of everyone here in their underwear," he whispered for her ears only. "We're all equal in our skin."

She moved her head back a little, and her gaze drifted up from his firm lips and into his blue eyes. Suddenly, equality took a dive. This man *had* no equal.

"Are you picturing me in my underwear yet?" he murmured, a gleam in those eyes, his head still close to hers, his cool, clean breath floating over her.

Her stomach quivered. "I—"

"Hey, Adam," a male voice interrupted. "Stop monopolizing the lady and introduce us."

Relieved at the interruption, Jenna glanced up to see a couple taking a seat at their table. The man was handsome and vaguely familiar, and the attractive blonde next to him was trying to hide her curiosity as she looked at Jenna. There was also something in the other woman's eyes…

"Hey, you have your own lady to monopolize, Todd," Adam joked, casually slipping his arm around Jenna in a proprietary gesture. So this was Todd and Chelsea. Adam appeared to be relaxed, but Jenna could feel the sudden tension in his body, and she realized this was his way of keeping the other couple at a physical distance. No doubt he didn't want to encourage Chelsea by kissing her hello, either.

But Chelsea took it into her own hands. "Adam, how *are* you?" she said, leaning down and giving him a kiss on the cheek. His lower cheek. Nearer his mouth. Jenna felt his arm tighten against her back.

He introduced her then, and Jenna became conscious of who these people actually were. Ordinary people? Not on your life. Todd was the son of a well-known real estate giant, and Chelsea's father was in steel. Wealth dripped from their family trees like liquid gold.

Good God, what had she gotten herself mixed up in? She'd known the Roths were a part of the upper classes, so she should have expected his best friends would be, as well. Now she had to pretend she was one of them. Could she do it? She glanced at Chelsea and saw that gleam in her eyes, and Jenna knew she'd give it a darn good try.

Thankfully, she didn't have to sit next to the other woman. Unfortunately, the round table gave them a clear view of each other and didn't put half as much distance between Chelsea and herself as she'd like.

After that, talk at the table was limited as a constant stream of people who came up to chat with the dignitaries. This was followed by a delicious three-course dinner, interspersed by speeches, some long, some short, some downright boring.

And polite society was…well…polite.

"So, Jenna," Chelsea said, as all the fanfare died down. "Do you live here in Melbourne?"

Jenna was just finishing the last of a dessert she didn't know how to pronounce but that was out of this world. Her appetite lost now, she nodded and kept her face blank as the inquisition began. The band had started up in the background with soft dance music but not enough to put a stop to any conversation.

Chelsea tilted her head. "I haven't seen you around before. What do you do?"

No doubt in Chelsea's crowd, a person usually *did* things that didn't involve employment. In *her* world, a person worked to survive. "I'm a jewelry designer."

"Oh?" Chelsea's gaze flicked to the necklace, but all she said was, "How lovely. Anyone we know?"

"I'm afraid not." No need to tell her she worked for Conti's. The less Chelsea knew about her, the easier things would be. Besides, it was obvious now that the other woman wasn't about to admire her design in front of the men.

Meoww...

Chelsea gave a false laugh. "Silly me. I guess if we knew your designs, then I wouldn't need to ask who you work for."

Todd looked on his wife with affection. "You're not silly, darling. You're very sweet."

"Oh, Todd," she murmured, but Jenna noticed she didn't actually look him in the eye.

Todd winked at Adam. "Don't you think my wife is sweet, Adam?" There was nothing in his glance that said he suspected anything amiss between his wife and his best friend.

Adam smiled. "Very sweet, Todd." Then he stood up and held his hand out to Jenna. "Excuse me, but I want to dance with my lady," he said, before leading her out to the middle of the floor, where he gathered her up against him, his hard body melding her curves.

Her pulse gave a rapid thud and she drew back, pretending to look up into his face but mainly needing to *not* be quite so close. "She's got it bad for you, Adam."

"Thanks. Just what I *didn't* need to hear."

"Sorry, but that woman is saccharine sweet."

"Yeah, and I'm definitely not into sweet things." One corner of his mouth lifted. "It's why I like you so much."

She had to smile. "You say such nice things to a girl."

He chuckled, his blue eyes amused. "Keep smiling, Jenna."

She reminded herself this was merely for their audience. "Like this?" she said, flashing him a brilliant smile.

He looked down at her. "Not quite. Make it dreamier. Like you mean it."

"Ahh, playacting, you mean?"

"*Now* you're getting the hang of it."

They shared another smile. A warm one this time. Then without warning his gaze slid downward and trailed along the cleave of her breasts like slow-moving fingertips. She could feel herself blush as her smile dissolved.

"Good. That's very convincing," he murmured. "Now you're acting like we're sharing an intimate moment."

She stiffened. "Am I?"

"Relax. You're spoiling it."

Her head went back farther. "*Me?* You're the one who's taking this to another level."

He pressed his hand against her upper back, guiding her head closer to his shoulder. "Shh. We look like we're arguing. Pretend you're whispering sweet nothings in my ear."

She didn't care what they looked like right then. This wasn't about acting for the others. This was about him taking advantage of the moment. "I'm not sweet, remember? And I don't *do* sweet nothings."

"Chelsea's watching us," he said softly.

"Tough."

A second ticked by before he warned silkily, "Don't forget our deal, Ms. Branson."

She caught her breath. "Don't forget Stewart" was what he was really saying. It was on the tip of her tongue to remind him of his own brother, Liam, but tit for tat wouldn't wash with him right now. It would be unwise of her not to take heed. She had to look at the bigger picture and not spoil all they'd accomplished this evening.

Somehow she forced herself to relax as she looked over his shoulder at the other dancing couples.

"That's better," he said, after a minute or two.

She immediately pulled back her head to look at him, not wanting him to think she was a timid little mouse who did what he told her to do. "By the way, why didn't you tell me who Todd and Chelsea were? I didn't know I'd have to deal with such affluent people."

He looked surprised. "I didn't think it mattered."

"It doesn't," she lied. "But it would have been nice to have been forewarned."

"You're doing well. Don't let them intimidate you." He leaned his head back to look down at her. "Remember the underwear trick," he said, giving a devilish smile.

She rolled her eyes, but she was trying *not* to think about Adam stripped down to his underwear. She automatically knew he wouldn't wear boxer shorts. No, this man would wear men's briefs, unashamedly revealing to a woman how much he could want her. The thought made her feel warmish and light-headed.

The music ended right then, and they returned to their table. She suspected her flushed cheeks would tell the others how Adam affected her, but thankfully his attention was diverted by another couple.

Jenna grabbed her purse and headed for the powder room, needing some breathing space for herself. Her cheeks had cooled by the time she sat on a stool and tucked some loose strands of hair back into her chignon. She was refreshing her lipstick in the large mirror when Chelsea entered the room. She smothered a groan. This was just what she didn't need.

The woman smiled at her as she slid onto the stool next to Jenna and started to fluff up her hair. A few more seconds then, "You and Adam look like a pair of lovebirds," she said casually, her gaze sliding across to Jenna in the mirror.

Jenna put her lipstick away as she fought to keep her expression happy. "Do we?"

"I must admit I was surprised to see you with him." Chelsea tidied another strand of her hair. "He's been going out with another woman for quite some time now."

Jenna managed to hide her surprise. Adam could have at least prepared her for that. "These things happen." She picked up her purse, about to get to her feet.

"How long have you known him?" Chelsea asked, applying some blusher now.

Jenna stayed sitting, all at once curious how far this woman was prepared to go. "Long enough," she said, giving a private little smile, seeing a flash of dismay in the other woman's eyes. "And you? How long have you known Adam, Chelsea?"

Chelsea recovered quickly. "Almost a year," she cooed. "We're still just getting to know each other."

Jenna was slightly taken aback. If she *had* been involved with Adam, she'd be quite upset by this woman's intimations. "What does that mean?" she said coolly, telling herself she was only playing a part but determined not to let this woman run roughshod over her anyway.

Chelsea blinked. "Er…nothing." She seemed horrified, almost as if she hadn't expected to be caught out. And that was probably more true than not. Who would challenge an heiress very often?

Jenna watched her pick up her purse and hurry into one of the cubicles, closing the door behind her, but she had to wonder why the woman hadn't known she was being obvious—to other people if not to her husband. Was Chelsea's world totally without accountability?

After that there was more socializing, with other people dropping by their table. Chelsea was quieter than before, and she avoided talking directly to Jenna, though her eyes would sneak to Adam whenever she thought no one was watching.

The evening slowly wound down and Jenna found she was tired of being constantly on show. She wasn't sure she'd like this life.

"Would you like to go home now?" Adam said quite loudly during a break in conversation, and though relieved, she knew he wanted others to think they were going "home" together.

"Oh, you can't!" Chelsea exclaimed, before Jenna could reply. "Come back to our place for a drink, Adam. Please."

Todd nodded. "Yes, good idea. You both should come back to our place for a nightcap. Or we can go to the casino for a few hours, if you like."

Jenna swallowed a groan. No, she didn't like. She wanted to go home to her own bed. To sleep. And to forget about these people, if only temporarily.

Adam shook his head. "Thanks, but it's getting late and Jenna and I have a full weekend coming up." He smiled at Jenna like she was the be-all and end-all of his existence.

"Oh, but—" Chelsea began.

"Darling," Todd said, putting his hand on his wife's arm. "They want to be alone."

Chelsea's face went blank. "Oh."

Todd laughed. "Don't tell me you've forgotten how that

feels?" He smiled musingly at the others. "How soon they forget."

For the first time, Jenna had the feeling that Todd was putting on a show. She didn't know why. His smile was as bright as before, his attitude as easygoing. There was just a hint of something...something deep in his eyes perhaps....

They all got up from the table together, then left in separate limousines. As they drove off, Adam pressed a button and the screen slid open. "Harry, go straight to my place," he instructed, putting his hand on Jenna's arm to silence her when she went to speak.

"Yes, Mr. Roth." The screen slid shut.

Her stomach fluttered. "I want to go home, Adam," she said firmly. This wasn't part of the deal.

"Chelsea and Todd are behind us."

"What!" She sat up straighter and twisted around. The white limousine was behind them. "Are they following us?"

"No. Their path home goes right past my apartment building. It's just our bad luck that they left at the same time as we did."

She glanced at him suspiciously in the passing street-lights, but he didn't seem to be hiding anything. "I'll catch a cab home from your place then."

"Harry will take you after you have a nightcap."

"I'd prefer to go straight home as soon as we get there." Was he up to something after all?

His eyes fixed on her. "Are you scared of coming up to my apartment?"

"No."

"Scared of me?"

"No." And if she was, she would never admit it.

He studied her, then appeared to accept her answer.

"Look, Chelsea and Todd are night owls. They could be driving around looking for someplace to go. I don't want them to see you in a cab, and I don't want to risk them seeing you inside this limo alone, either." She opened her mouth. "Yeah, even with tinted windows. It's best you wait at my place for a while. Give them time to get settled somewhere."

"Are you making this up as you go along?"

He chuckled. "No." Then he sobered. "I wish the hell I was. I know it all sounds unlikely, but just humor me this once."

She thought about that. It really was no use taking a risk, no matter how slight. And while she didn't like to think Adam would go back on his word, he might well decide to do nothing just yet about the money for Stewart. Not until she'd "paid" her dues.

In full.

She inclined her head. "I suppose I could have a small nightcap with you."

"Good."

They drove awhile. It was almost midnight and being a Friday night, St. Kilda Road was still flowing with traffic and people strolling along the streets, but she and Adam may as well have been the only ones around. Jenna could feel him on the seat next to her…could see the length of his thighs beneath the dark trousers…could inhale the scent of his aftershave…. His presence disturbed her.

She glanced at him, needing to break the silence. "Chelsea said you've been seeing another woman."

His lips firmed into a straight line. "It was over a few weeks ago."

It was hard to tell if he was annoyed with *her* for mentioning it, with Chelsea for telling her or with the other woman. Probably all three.

"She needs to get up-to-date then," Jenna reflected.

"She needs more than that," he muttered, for a moment looking like a man who'd had more than enough. His face hardened again. "Chelsea befriended Diane, who won't admit it's over between us. Unfortunately, Diane—that's the lady I was going out with—unwittingly keeps her informed. Diane has no idea Chelsea is using her for her own purposes."

She tilted her head back. "Boy, your life is a real mess, isn't it?"

He grimaced. "Yes, but not through any fault of my own." Then he gave a shrug. "All this goes with the territory, I'm afraid."

"Territory? Being a Roth, you mean?"

"Being a man," he drawled, his sense of humor reappearing.

She laughed, then suddenly a car horn blasted a good-night from Todd and Chelsea, making Jenna jump, and the white limousine went zooming past just as they arrived at the front of Adam's apartment building.

"Make yourself comfortable while I pour us that night-cap," he said, once they stepped out of the private elevator upstairs.

Jenna put her purse down on the couch and strolled onto the balcony. She wasn't planning on making herself too comfortable, certainly not in the way he might mean.

He followed her soon after, and they stood there sipping brandy and looking out on a warm autumn night that still held strong traces of summer. The building wasn't particularly high, but it was prestigious and on the main thoroughfare. From what she could tell the last time she was here, the whole of the top floor was his penthouse, with a sweeping panoramic view of the city, the bay and the mountain range in the distance.

Of course the last time she was here on the balcony, Adam had been standing much too close for her liking. She looked at him now and found him watching her with a flame flickering in those dark depths. Her breath caught high in her throat. He'd loosened his tie and he looked incredibly sexy.

"That color suits you," he murmured.

Nervously, she said the first thing that came to mind. "Vinnie's has some great things."

A crease formed between his eyebrows. "Vinnie's? I don't think I've heard of them."

She couldn't help herself. She laughed. "St. Vincent de Paul. You know, they run a lot of the secondhand stores."

His expression faltered. "You're wearing a *used* dress?"

"Unheard of in your world, no doubt," she said, oddly not taking offense. He really didn't know any better. "It's clean and they have some great stuff. Seriously, lots of people buy secondhand goods from them. It works out well all around. People have decent clothes to wear that they might not be able to afford, and the money goes back into charity."

He stood there looking at her as if she was speaking another language, and she laughed again at his confusion. This guy had no idea of the real world. Not everyone could afford caviar and champagne.

Out of the blue, his gaze intensified on her face, then dropped down to her lips. The flame returned to his eyes. She could feel her smile slip away as he slowly brought his head toward her. She couldn't seem to move, not even to put aside the glass she cradled in her hands.

He placed his lips on hers and stilled, and it was the most incredible thing she'd ever experienced. He didn't touch her with anything but his mouth, yet he was oddly touching her in other ways she didn't want to think about. How was this happening?

And then his brandy tongue nudged her lips open. She didn't resist. She couldn't, and he began long, mesmerizing slides over her. He did it in right measures too, not to tease, but exploring her...just right...so right...mouth-to-mouth as his warm breath shimmied through her, holding her suspended in time...until the moment she'd be able to take a breath on her own again.

He slowly drew back, a watchful expression about him. She took that first breath then, aware something had clicked between them. A blink later, his eyes filled with male satisfaction. Jenna stiffened, not wanting him to get the wrong impression here. She wasn't available for long kisses that lingered.

"I should slap your face."

"Mmm, kinky."

Her chin rose. "Just because I *didn't* slap your face doesn't mean I'll let you get away with it again."

Challenge flared in his eyes, then banked, his sensual mouth curving upward. "In other words, you don't want to be my mistress and I'd better not expect you to be?"

"Exactly."

"Fair enough."

She managed a snort. What the hell was he playing at?

He arched a brow. "You look surprised."

"I am. I didn't expect you'd give up so easily."

"Who said I had?" He smiled...but a moment later it was gone. "Stay the night."

"Wh-what? Didn't we just agree—"

"It's getting late. You can sleep in the spare room."

She searched his face, not sure what she was looking for precisely. "Is all this really necessary, Adam?"

"Unfortunately, yes. It's only just occurred to me, but I

wouldn't be surprised if Chelsea appears on my doorstep tomorrow morning to see if you're still here."

Unease rippled through Jenna. "There's a name for this. It's called stalking."

"It's beginning to appear that way, yet I really have no proof of anything. Every time she calls me, or even if she were to come here tomorrow, she has Todd as her excuse. Nothing she does right now would hold up in court." He grimaced. "Not that I want it to get that far."

"Maybe you might need to say something to Todd?" She wasn't sure why, but she didn't mention her suspicions that Todd might be aware of something going on with Chelsea.

"Not yet. Hopefully having you around will make her come to her senses."

"And if it doesn't?"

"I'll worry about that if it happens."

All at once, any arguments for going home didn't seem so important. She put her glass down on the small table. "I think I'd like to go to bed now," she said, then schooled her features, trying not to show how intimate that sounded.

He merely nodded, looking pleased that she was staying. "I'll find you something to sleep in."

"Thank you." She waited for him to comment, surprised when he didn't take the opportunity to make some sort of sexy remark.

"But do me a favor," he finally said. "Don't put the light on in the bedroom, just in case."

She lifted a brow. "In case?"

"In case Todd and Chelsea see it. They know the penthouse. They can see it from the road." A pulse ticked in his temple. "Bloody hell! I hate living like this."

In spite of everything, she had to have some sympathy

for him. He was used to living in a media fishbowl, but no doubt he'd always been able to rely on his close friends.

Until now.

Now his closest friend and wife were the very ones he had to keep at arm's length.

It was strange having a woman spend the night in his apartment and not in his bed, Adam mused, returning to the balcony after showing Jenna to the spare room and pouring himself another small measure of brandy. In the darkness he took a seat on the lounger until his skin cooled under the late-night breeze. It was no use going to his room and undressing. Not yet. Not with thoughts of Jenna slipping his T-shirt over her head and down her delicious body, as she would be doing right this minute.

Groaning, he told himself to push the thought to the side, but it was darn hard pushing any thoughts about Jenna to the side. She was so beautiful and had looked gorgeous in that gown tonight, whether it was secondhand or not. She'd been such an asset at the ball, holding her own with everyone, including Chelsea…including *him*. He hadn't had such an enjoyable time with a woman for a long time, especially at these affairs, where everyone was someone and no one fully relaxed from being on show.

And yet being around Jenna could never relax a man. Not unless it was in the aftermath of making love to her, and even then he suspected he'd want her again immediately too much to relax. Hell, after kissing her twice tonight, and after dancing with her, he didn't just suspect it. He *knew* he would want her again right away. No question.

God, he'd better stop thinking about her or he'd never get to bed. He needed all the sleep he could get, not just because she was in his apartment tonight, but with her being in his life for the next month. He had the feeling he was going to be sleep deprived from now on. Whether he was sexually deprived, too, was up to Jenna.

And at least there was one thing. Jenna was keeping his worries about Chelsea at bay. And that meant she was serving her purpose.

He'd chosen well.

Four

Jenna had undressed by the light of the city last night as Adam had asked, so she awoke the next morning to the full sun streaming through the glass panes. It was Saturday, but this wasn't like her usual Saturdays. She normally didn't wake in an unfamiliar bed in the apartment of a man she barely knew, wearing that man's shirt. A man it was wise to keep at a distance.

The very thought had her tossing back the blankets and sliding out of the sheets, the T-shirt she'd slipped into last night after Adam had left the room grazing her thigh. He hadn't commented on the balcony, but as he'd handed her one of his shirts, the look in his eyes said he was fully aware of what she'd be wearing to bed.

Warmth stole under her skin at the memory.

Then she spotted her evening gown draped over a chair, and reality returned. There was nothing worse than waking up and realizing you had to dress in yesterday's clothes.

At least she'd had the forethought to wash out her panties before going to bed last night, and they were now wearable again.

In the guest bathroom she showered, then brushed her teeth with a new toothbrush she found in the vanity cabinet. Thankfully she had some makeup in her purse, and she began to feel more human as she slipped her own clothes back on. After that she went to look for Adam in the main living area. If he wasn't about, she'd leave a note and take a cab home. She rather hoped he'd gone out.

It was interesting that she didn't see any photographs of Adam's late wife around the place. As much as he was in the public eye, she was discovering he was a very private person. Of course grief was a very private thing after all, she thought. She remembered hearing of the accident and thinking it a tragedy, but never in a million years would she have believed she'd meet the man, let alone pretend to be his mistress and wake up in his apartment. Life had certainly taken a turn she hadn't expected.

Nor needed.

Adam was at the breakfast bar, eating cereal and fresh fruit. He looked fresh enough to eat himself, and so damn handsome, but she pretended not to notice as she placed her purse on the coffee table.

He looked up, observed her deep blue evening dress, and furnished her a lazy smile. "Ahh, the morning after."

"Exactly," she said with a grimace.

"Yet you still manage to look gorgeous."

"A little bleary-eyed this morning, aren't we?" she mocked.

He laughed. "Did you sleep well?"

"As well as could be expected." It was amazing she'd slept at all, considering the circumstances.

"I hope you didn't feel the need to lock your door?"

"Actually, no, I didn't." She figured that if he'd been going to make a move on her, he would have pressed for more during that kiss on his balcony.

God help her, but she'd never drink brandy again without thinking of it. Of him. She was doomed to forever remember.

"Did Chelsea turn up, by any chance?" she asked. It *had* been the reason he'd asked her to sleep here last night.

His whole face became hard-edged again. "No, thank heavens. She's the last thing I need." Then he visibly forced himself to relax with a smile. "And now…about today. Are you doing anything special?"

She was suddenly wary. "It depends."

"I have to go to the Carlton Gardens this afternoon. My family is sponsoring a gardening exhibit at the Melbourne International Flower and Garden Show and I said I'd drop by while my parents are out of town. I'd like you to come with me. We can take a walk around the gardens afterward. It's quite something."

Jenna could see her leisure time over the next month being swallowed up by him and his engagements. "You didn't think to mention this before?"

His brow furrowed. "Don't you have anything to wear? We'll stop by one of the boutiques."

She made a dismissive gesture. "No, that's not the problem."

"You don't like flowers?"

"I love flowers, but that's not the point. I didn't think all this was going to take up so much of my time."

His mouth tightened. "No, the point is that it's a good idea to be seen together again after last night. It'll put us in other people's minds as a couple."

His words sank in and she sighed heavily. "I guess so."

"Your enthusiasm becomes you," he drawled.

She ignored that as her eye caught sight of the newspaper beside him. "Is there anything in that about the ball?" she said a little anxiously as she moved a few feet farther toward him.

"No. There's some pictures, but we managed to miss out this time."

"Good." Her parents and her sister-in-law might have known about her date last night, but she was still glad not to have her and Adam's picture splashed across the papers. She really wasn't interested in that kind of notoriety.

He frowned. "I assume your question means you haven't told your parents about me then?"

"I told them," she said, disabusing him of the idea. "But only about the ball. They don't know about Stewart and the money." She realized instantly her mistake in saying too much. She pulled a face. "Darn. I shouldn't have told you that."

A hint of steel momentarily glinted in his eyes. "We're in the same boat, remember. My parents don't know about it, either."

"That's true," she said, clamping down on her anxiety. They might be able to destroy each other's families, but in an odd twist, their only guarantees in protecting them were each other.

All at once he lifted his foot and drew the stool out from beside him. "Come and eat some breakfast," he said, and suddenly the focus was back on the moment again.

On them.

She looked at him, looked at the stool. If she sat down he would be right next to her. "Thanks, but I'm not really hungry."

"You'll need something in your stomach for the afternoon. You don't want to be light-headed and faint. Then you *will* be in the papers," he joked, but she had the feeling he knew why she didn't want to sit beside him.

She slid onto the stool, determined to show he didn't frighten her. "Perhaps I'll just have some fresh fruit."

"Help yourself." He indicated the platter of sliced fruit then lifted the coffeepot in a silent gesture.

She nodded. "Thanks. Did you fix all this yourself?" Somehow she couldn't see him in a kitchen peeling and slicing fruit for too long. This man belonged in the boardroom—her pulse fluttered—and the bedroom.

"No. I have a housekeeper."

Jenna concentrated on forking slices of mango and pineapple onto her plate, but she was wondering if the housekeeper had known there was someone sleeping in the spare room last night.

"Yes."

She blinked, then glanced up at Adam. "What?"

He shot her an amused glance. "Yes, my housekeeper knew someone was sleeping in the other bedroom. I had to leave her a note so she wouldn't disturb you."

He'd read her mind again. Was he clairvoyant, or was she being too obvious? She hoped it wasn't the latter.

"That would have been a novelty for her then. I'm sure the spare room doesn't get used too often around here."

He laughed softly. "Oh, yeah, you're right about that."

She couldn't help it. A smile pulled at her lips. "A novelty for you too, I imagine."

"Double 'oh, yeah.'"

She chuckled and so did he. And then his eyes snagged hers. She felt like she was being pulled into them…willingly drowning….

"Er…" She dragged herself back from the brink. "Where's your housekeeper now? Is she still here?" She'd concentrate on this.

He took a moment to answer. "She's gone to Vic Market. She wanted to get some fresh food."

Queen Victoria Market was the premier open-air market, brimming with Old World charm, but right now Jenna was having trouble getting past the husky *charm* of this man's voice.

She took a breath and focused. She assumed the woman didn't live here. That would definitely cramp Adam's style.

And then a sudden thought struck her.

"How well do you know her, Adam? I mean, if Chelsea got to Diane then she could probably get to your housekeeper. Then she might tell Chelsea we didn't sleep together last night. She could do it inadvertently."

He was shaking his head before she'd finished speaking. "No, that wouldn't happen. Sheryl has been with me for ten years. I trust her implicitly." His voice said he was firm on this. No doubts at all.

She held his gaze. With his family being in the limelight it would be hard to trust people. For him to trust his housekeeper was saying something. "I'm glad."

After they finished breakfast, Adam had to take a couple of calls and she knew it was a good time to leave. He phoned his driver to come and get her.

"Be ready at one," he said. "Harry will collect you then."

Jenna was ready as planned, dressed in a sleeveless linen dress topped with a summery jacket. She told herself it wasn't like she was the queen or anything. This was just a business event, just like her dealings with Adam were business when it came right down to it.

Still, she was nervous. If she hadn't been with Adam, she'd have worn her good pair of jeans and sneakers and roamed around the gardens with a girlfriend. Maybe she'd have even taken Vicki and the girls, or gone with her parents. Her mother and father both liked this sort of thing.

Adam must have sensed her anxiety. "Don't stress out," he whispered, as he walked her along one of the many paths in the Carlton Gardens, through an explosion of colorful exhibits and displays, toward the historic Royal Exhibition Building.

She was grateful for his arm inside the Great Hall as quite a few high profile people stopped to talk to him. The one thing she did notice now—as she had last night—was that people treated you differently when you were with a Roth. No wonder the Roth men thought they were God's gift to women. No wonder Liam had thought he was beyond reproach.

It was late afternoon before they could leave to take a walk around the outside exhibits spread over the glorious gardens. Thankfully she'd had the sense to wear comfortable, low-heeled yet stylish shoes, but trust a man not to think about her walking in high heels, she mused, as they strolled through a world of flowers and scents, past historic fountains and ornamental lakes. She glanced at him and saw him walking with his jacket thrown over his shoulder. He looked like a model for a magazine advertisement.

He caught her eye and she looked away. "The weather's perfect today," she said, pretending to admire the creativity of the exhibits, pretending *not* to notice how terrific he looked or the arm that snaked around her waist and pulled her close even as they walked. It was for show, she told herself.

"Are you glad you came?" he asked, smiling down at her.

She nodded. "Yes, I am actually." Now the formalities were over, she meant it. The fresh air, the warm sunshine and the man beside her were potent stuff. She wasn't silly enough to let down her guard completely, but for the moment, the stroll in the afternoon sunshine was making her feel pleasantly lazy.

Later as they were finally leaving the gardens, he said, "How about we go for a drink at the casino? We could have an early dinner in one of their restaurants after that."

It sounded wonderful but… "I really should go home."

"Why?"

"Do I need an excuse?" she asked, but her voice lacked conviction.

"Yes."

She smiled and he smiled back, and suddenly she knew she was in danger of completely letting her guard down today. She couldn't afford that.

She gave a shake of her head. "It's best I go home."

"Best for whom? Have dinner with me, Jenna, otherwise I'll have to dine alone." He stepped in front of her, making her stop walking. "Besides, I can't ask anyone else. Word might get back to Chelsea."

She was grateful for the young child that ran into them right then. Adam's words were a reminder that she couldn't let herself soften toward this man. For a moment she'd forgotten that their being together was for Stewart's sake, on her part at least.

"Jenna?" he reminded her, once the mother had rescued her child, leaving them alone in a dwindling crowd of people heading for the exit gates.

She faked a smile. "Okay, why not?"

He must have sensed the subtle difference in her attitude because his eyes narrowed slightly, but she didn't give him the chance to talk. She stepped around him and continued walking, and he fell into step beside her.

They ended up playing roulette at the casino for a couple

of hours. Jenna wasn't a big gambler but surprisingly she enjoyed it. Her ex-boyfriend, Lewis, had brought her here a couple of times and had once got himself half-drunk and caused a small scene. Being with Adam was different. He had total control of himself, and he seemed delighted in her excitement when she won a small amount at the table.

Around seven they strolled up the stunning black marble staircase to one of the lavish restaurants, the sound of the fountains near the entrance echoing high up the stairs. It was early and the restaurant was just starting to fill up, but the maître d' knew Adam and welcomed him with deference, then took them to an intimate table in the corner. No doubt Adam had brought many women here. But Jenna wasn't really one of them, and that was another reminder this was all a farce. One she shouldn't forget. She was wallpaper for him, that's all.

Adam nodded to someone at a table across the room, then smiled back at Jenna like she was his everything. "Good. Word should get back to Chelsea now."

She smiled tightly. "Perfect."

They ordered the meal, and once alone again he gave her another smile. "I've enjoyed spending time with you today, Jenna."

She knew this was an act for the benefit of others. "It was a nice day," was all she could manage.

His gaze rested on her. "I mean it."

She tried to steady her breathing. "Don't get comfortable with me, Adam. I'm only here with you because of my brother."

He leaned back farther in his chair, his mouth thinning slightly. "Ahh, bring it all back to that. It's good protection."

"I don't need protection from you. I can handle myself."

"Don't challenge me, Jenna."

She wanted to dare him, but something...the way he narrowed his eyes...said he was waiting for her to do just that and he didn't care right then that they were in a roomful of people.

"I wouldn't give you the satisfaction," she said, pasting on a smile when she saw the waiter returning with their drinks.

After a delicious meal that she couldn't do justice to, he took her home at a fairly early hour, insisting on walking her to her door. She felt obliged to invite him in for coffee, but her tone said she'd prefer he didn't accept.

He accepted.

"You have a nice apartment," he said, as she put the coffeepot on.

"Thanks." She turned away, concentrating on preparing the brew. He'd been here last night before the ball, though he hadn't looked at anything but her.

And then there had been that kiss....

"You own it?"

She hoped he thought the flush in her cheeks was from annoyance. "Now is that a polite question to ask?"

"I doubt I was trying to be polite," he mused.

"Yes, I forgot who I was talking to for a minute there," she scoffed, then admitted, "Yes, it's mine."

No need to tell him the loan was almost killing her in repayments. Her job paid well, but interest rates had gone up recently. If only she'd known Stewart was going to need money *before* she'd put her life savings down as a deposit. She would have rented for a while longer until her brother was paid back the money owed to him by the Roths.

She shook off her thoughts, and they had their coffee while Adam told her a story about an interior decorator he'd dated who'd once painted huge daisies on his living-room wall—in bright orange.

"You didn't like it?" Jenna joked.

His lips twisted. "There's a moral to the story. Don't break up with a woman until she's finished the decorating." He drained his cup and put it down on the table. "Now, it's Sunday tomorrow. What will you be doing?"

"Absolutely nothing." She'd already decided tomorrow was her own. "And I intend to keep it that way. Surely we can give the issue of the money a rest for one day?"

He stared hard and for a moment she thought he might argue.

Her chin lifted. "I need some time to myself, Adam," she added, not to soften him, but merely to point out why she wouldn't back down.

He took a moment to nod, then he pushed to his feet. "Okay. I understand."

She blinked in surprise. "You do?"

"We all need space sometimes." He leaned toward her, kissed her cheek and headed for the door. "I'll call you." He shut the door quietly behind him.

She was alone.

"I'm sure you will," she murmured in the silent apartment.

On Monday morning Adam was just finishing up some work when Dominic's personal assistant announced Todd was there to see him. He groaned inwardly. His friend didn't stop by the Roth offices too often. "Send him in, thanks, Janice."

Todd strolled in, looking the easygoing but confident businessman. "I see you're still doing Dominic's job."

"He's not due back from his honeymoon for another ten days."

Todd shook his head in bemusement. "Your brother only got married a couple of months ago and already he's taking another honeymoon. Sounds like things are turning out well for him."

Adam agreed. Yet it hadn't been so easy for his older brother. "I know, but things were…awkward between him and Cassandra at first. Now they've found they love each other, they wanted some time alone together with Nicole."

Todd's face sobered. "Yeah, I know. Liam's death certainly made an impact on everyone." His friend didn't know the half of it, Adam mused, knowing he couldn't tell him about Liam's involvement with Stewart Branson. The less anyone knew the better. "So I'm helping Dad run the show. He and Mum should be back from Brisbane tomorrow, as well."

"Good. That'll give you a clear weekend coming up."

Adam grew wary. "Why?"

"Chelsea and I are having a housewarming party at our new vacation home in the Grampians. We want you to come for the weekend. I assume you'll bring Jenna. Actually, Chelsea *insists* on you bringing her. Chels really liked her."

Adam had to bite his tongue. "Did she?"

"You know how Chels is. When she takes a liking to someone she almost kills them with kindness."

Adam *really* had to bite his tongue. "Yes, I know."

Todd looked pleased. "So you and Jenna will come?"

"I'm not sure," he began, seeing disappointment dawn in his friend's eyes. "Jenna may have something else planned," he said, more to give himself time to think about this. Spending a whole weekend with him might tip Chelsea over the edge, and that thought was far from egotistical.

"You and Jenna *have* to come, Adam," Todd said quickly,

then grimaced. "I think Chelsea needs to be around people she likes right now."

Adam went on full alert. "Why?"

Todd shrugged. "She's been a bit down lately."

"About?" God, if Chelsea had put her marriage at risk…

He seemed to hesitate. "She's had some…problems. It's just women's stuff, but you know how it goes."

Adam had the feeling there was something more to this, though suddenly he didn't get the impression it had anything to do with *him*. Thank God! Were Todd and Chelsea having marriage problems? Was the openness between them simply for show?

Todd cleared his throat. "I'd really like you there, Adam."

Adam considered his friend. If this was important to Todd, then he'd go. He nodded. "I'll see what I can do."

Todd's relief was evident.

After he left, Adam sat at the desk and twirled the gold pen in his fingers. He remembered Todd coming around to his apartment after Maddie died, making sure he was okay, then forcing him to get up and get dressed, forcing him to eat. Todd had been there for him every day when he'd been at the lowest point of his life. No one else had been able to get through to him. Todd had been the only one.

All at once he knew that even if there was something going on between Todd and Chelsea now, he wouldn't tell Jenna just yet. Otherwise she might think that he'd accept her as his companion for less than the agreed month. Whether the money issue was resolved between them soon or not, whether the issue with Chelsea was resolved quicker than expected, he still wanted to have his full month with Jenna Branson. And that's what he would have.

* * *

"Well, well, you're a dark horse, aren't you?" Marco Conti murmured, coming into the room where Jenna was working on Monday morning.

She tried not to react to the slimy glint in his eyes. How on earth Roberto and Carmen Conti had parented such a son, she didn't know. Love was certainly blind in this case. In their minds, Marco could do no wrong.

"What do you mean, Marco?" she asked, picking up a small pair of pliers and continuing working.

"First you dump me at the races last weekend, and then I hear you attended the Mayoral Ball with none other than Adam Roth. *Then* I hear you were seen at the flower show with him on Saturday."

"So?" This guy had been busy.

"There's more to you than meets the eye, *cara mia.*"

She looked up. "Marco, who I go out with is none of your business. And I didn't dump you at the races. I *wasn't* your date."

Something dark crossed his face, then vanished. "You could do worse than catching a Roth."

"I don't think Adam would appreciate that comment," she said without thinking, and was surprised to see Marco cringe.

He recovered and gave a smarmy smile. "I was only joking, Jenna. That's all I was doing." A tiny pause. "You have no need to tell him what I said."

So…Marco was actually intimidated by something. Interesting.

Jenna could care less. She just wanted Marco out of her hair. "No, he doesn't need to know." An impish urge took hold of her. "But I'd appreciate if any gossip you hear you don't pass on here at work. I don't want people to feel awkward with me. I'm sure Adam would appreciate knowing you're helping me."

Marco drew himself up. "Of course."

She breathed a deep sigh of relief when he left. Not only had she got him off her back, but to him he had saved face by conceding to a Roth. She felt pleased with herself to have outwitted him.

Her self-congratulations didn't last, though, not when everything seemed to keep coming back to Adam. She was on edge about her next "gig" with him, whenever that would be. No doubt she would have to accompany him to a whole series of events he needed to attend over the coming weeks.

It didn't help that her mother had called yesterday morning to ask if she'd enjoyed the Mayoral Ball. Jenna had tried to sound enthused, while evading saying too much about the man she'd attended with. It hadn't helped that her parents had been about to head out to the flower show, which left no option but to admit she'd been the day before. With Adam? Yes, Jenna had replied. The brief silence that had come down the line had been telling, and she'd hurriedly reminded her mother not to say anything to Stewart.

This was all getting very trying very fast. Please God, let the money be settled soon. Then she'd be able to break it off with Adam, and her parents wouldn't be too concerned if she told them he hadn't been the one for her, and that would be the end of it.

Around seven-thirty that evening, Adam dropped by her apartment. He didn't kiss her hello, but her heart still thudded when she opened the door to him.

"Would you like to go out for a drink somewhere?" he asked, stepping inside.

She closed the door behind him. "Do I have to?" He

turned around with a wry look and she wrinkled her nose. "Sorry, I didn't mean it quite like that. I'm a working girl. I don't party during the week." Actually she didn't party much at all, not even on the weekends. She must be so different from his other women friends. *Mistresses,* she corrected, reminding herself that she wasn't his mistress and didn't intend to be, so being different in this case was a good thing.

A shadow of relief crossed his face. "That's okay. I'm not really up for it myself. I just thought *you* might like to go out."

His consideration softened something inside her, even more so when she saw that he looked tired. He must have a lot to worry about right now, with his brother and father away so much, not to mention all this business about Liam. She tried not to let it get to her.

"You've just finished work by the looks of things."

He loosened his tie a little. "Yes."

"Have you eaten?"

"Not yet."

She hesitated. "Me, either. I made spaghetti bolognese and there's plenty to share if you want to stay and eat with me. It's nothing fancy."

He eyed her quizzically. "You don't mind?"

"You've been feeding me a lot lately. I guess I can repay the favor," she said wryly.

He smiled. "With an invitation like that, how can I refuse?"

She smiled back at him, then spun toward the kitchen. "Would you like a glass of wine?" she asked, pleased that at least her voice sounded normal, even if her racing pulse wasn't.

He followed her and stood in the doorway. "No thanks. If

I had alcohol right now I'd probably fall asleep." His voice lingered. "Of course, then you'd have to put me to bed."

She peered at him, not smiling now. "Why do you say things like that? We don't have an audience."

"I like making you blush."

"I don't embarrass easily. If my cheeks are red, it's from anger," she fibbed.

The gleam in his eyes said he knew better. "I enjoy knowing I'm affecting a woman…like she affects me."

She felt heat burst into her cheeks. "Adam…" she warned.

"Do you realize you blush on and off for me? I kind of like being the switch that turns you on."

"And off," she flipped back at him. She handed him some cutlery and place mats. "Here. You can set the table over there."

He chuckled, then took the items and did as he was told. With a silent sigh of relief, she turned away and finished preparing the food. Soon they were sitting down to eat.

In contrast, Adam didn't talk much while they ate.

"That was delicious," he said, finally, putting his napkin aside after he'd cleaned his plate. Then he leaned back in his chair with an inward look. "You can be quite calming to be around."

"I can?"

His mouth tilted. "Sometimes."

"You're just tired."

He acknowledged that with a nod of his head. "I wanted to tell you something and was waiting until we'd eaten."

Her heart jumped into her throat. "You've got the money?" she said, hope rising inside her. It would solve all their problems if—

His mouth turned down at the corners. "No."

"Oh." That was somewhat disappointing, despite it still being early.

"My guys are on it now."

She nodded. It was a letdown to realize he'd kept to his word and hadn't even started looking for the money until she'd attended the ball with him. It said how much he *didn't* trust her. Of course, she didn't trust him either, so why would he be any different? There was nothing between them to trust anyway.

She held herself stiffly, preparing for what he was going to say. "What do you want to tell me then?"

"Todd stopped by my office to see me today. He and Chelsea are having a housewarming party this weekend. He wants us to come."

She considered that. "I guess it would be okay," she said slowly.

"It's in the Grampians, at their new vacation home."

"What!" She thought ahead. "That's a long drive."

"Around three hours. It'll mean staying overnight."

"In the same bedroom?"

"Yes."

"Same bed?"

"More than likely. Unless Chelsea decides to keep us apart and give us a room with twin beds, and that could be very likely," he said cynically. His gaze caught hold of her. "Would it be so awful sharing a bed with me?"

Her stomach rolled with nerves. "That's not the point, Adam."

"At least you don't deny you want me."

"I—"

"We're both adults, Jenna. We won't be hurting anyone if we take this further and sleep together."

"Making love was not part of our bargain." He was a man who'd have plenty of lovers. He had to realize by now that she didn't sleep around. "I'll come for the weekend, and I'll even share a room with you…" God help her. "But I'm *not* sleeping with you."

He gave an indifferent shrug. "Oh, well. I tried."

She didn't know if she was more disappointed that he had given up so easily, or dismayed that she was disappointed. Then she eyed him speculatively. Or had he given up? They still had to share a room together this weekend, didn't they? He was probably just playing with her.

Adam pushed to his feet. "I thought I'd drive us there myself on Saturday morning instead of Friday evening, and we can come back after lunch Sunday. That way we only have the one night to worry about sharing a bed." He smiled down at her. "Not that it's a worry to me."

After he left, Jenna lay awake until the early hours. She rather thought even one night with Adam Roth might be too much.

Way…too much.

Five

Jenna grew more apprehensive the closer they got to the Grampians National Park. She should be enjoying the richness of the deep blue sky and the picturesque rural view on either side of the highway, but being under Chelsea's watchful eyes at the Mayoral Ball a week ago had been exhausting. She couldn't shrug off the feeling that a weekend of Chelsea might prove too much.

"I'm not sure this is such a good idea, Adam."

He shot her a sideways glance. "Relax."

Relax? This wasn't just about Chelsea. With him looking so handsome in gray trousers and a black polo shirt, a woman would have to be dead to be able to relax next to him.

"Couldn't you have just told Todd no?" she had to point out. "Or said we had other plans? Perhaps you could have said you had to work. Better yet, that *I* had to work."

"You agreed to do this."

"I know, but—"

"Accept it, Jenna."

She sighed. "I suppose so."

Soon after, Adam needed a break from the driving so they stopped at a small café for coffee before getting back on the road again. They drove through historic gold-mining towns and the many wineries in the area, and the journey would have been exciting if her stomach hadn't been tied in knots. Not even the peekaboo glimpses of the Grampian Mountains in the distance eased her anxiety.

Finally, the mountains were growing closer and they were turning onto an unassuming dirt road outside one of the main towns. They traveled along it for a short distance before turning into an open gate sided by two stone pillars. The place was certainly secluded.

Jenna's eyes widened as she looked ahead to where the road ended about half a mile in the distance. "Good grief. That's their *vacation* home? That's a mansion with a capital *M*."

He looked faintly surprised. "They do a lot of entertaining."

She gave a hollow laugh. "So do lots of people, but not everyone has a vacation home like this. Most families are lucky to have one house, let alone two."

His jaw thrust forward. "I know it."

Something made her push. "I don't think you do." Undaunted, she continued, "Doesn't your family have a vacation home? Somewhere you get away from the city? Didn't I read that your family has a yacht?"

He didn't look pleased at the inquisition. "The *Lady Laura* is named after my mother." He paused. "And we have a vacation home in far north Queensland. It's on a secluded beach so that we can have some privacy."

"A tropical retreat," she mocked. "How nice. Everyone

should have one." She knew it was nerves, but she couldn't seem to stop herself from running off at the mouth.

He shot her a dark glare as he pulled up in front of the mansion. Then he cut the engine and turned to her fully. "You seem to have a problem with anyone who has money."

She went on the defensive. "When it's built on other people's money, I do."

His mouth tightened. "I know you're on edge, but do me a favor. Try not to pick an argument in front of the others."

"Or?"

"You won't like the result."

"Is that a—"

Adam's door flew open and Chelsea stuck her head in the car. "Welcome, Adam," she said, a glowing light of excitement in her eyes as she put her hand on his arm and practically pulled him from the seat.

Todd opened the passenger-side door. "Yes, welcome to our humble abode, Jenna," he said, smiling at her. "Here, let me help you out."

Jenna quickly pulled herself together and took advantage of his outstretched hand. "Thank you, Todd." Once on her feet, she glanced across the roof of the car and saw Chelsea hanging off Adam's arm like some sort of expensive accessory. Jenna had dressed in a pantsuit she thought was becoming, but up against Chelsea she felt like she should be ushering people to their seats. The only thing she was missing was a flashlight, she mused with self-derision.

Todd tucked Jenna's arm in his. "Did you have a good trip?" he asked, as the other two came around the car.

"Yes, it's a lovely drive in the country." She shot Adam a quick look that harked back to their conversation about the rich. His eyes narrowed in reply.

"Is everything okay?" Chelsea asked, evidently catching the tension in the air, looking from one to the other.

Adam smoothly extricated himself from Chelsea's clutches. "Jenna gets a little carsick at times," he explained. "Are you feeling better now, darling?" he asked with fake concern.

Jenna was sure Chelsea gave the tiniest start at the endearment, as she did herself. Goodness, if he was using endearments now she really *was* going to feel woozy.

She cleared her throat. "A little."

Chelsea soon recovered with a hopeful smile. "Perhaps you'd like to take a quick lie down before lunch then, Jenna? We won't eat for a few hours yet. We'll look after Adam, so don't you worry about that."

Jenna rather thought it was more Chelsea who would look after him. Still, she smiled gratefully and avoided Adam's eyes. "Yes, I think I *would* like to lie down," she said, needing some time away from him…from them…*all* of them. "That's if you really don't mind, Chelsea?"

The other woman beamed at her, friends for life right at this minute. "Of course not!" In one swift movement, Chelsea moved her husband aside and slipped her arm in Jenna's. "Some of the others arrived earlier, but don't feel obligated to rush. Take as long as you need."

In next to no time, they were inside the magnificent foyer and Jenna was handed over to the housekeeper. Then Chelsea and Todd took Adam off to another part of the house to meet the other guests. If she'd cared, Jenna would have smarted a little at being dumped so expertly. As it was, she could only be thankful that she was being shown to a suite with a sitting room plus a small private balcony, and that she had it to herself for now. It served Adam right for threatening her back there in the car.

Then she looked at the king-size bed.

Oh, heavens.

"Time for lunch, Jenna."

Jenna's eyelids flew open and she looked straight into Adam's eyes. She became instantly aware that his irises were blue and darker somehow. Had he been watching her? She blinked in panic and sat up, and he straightened away from the bed.

"You could have let me sleep longer," she grumbled, trying not to let him see how he affected her.

"No chance. You got away with sneaking in here before. Now I want you by my side."

She quirked an eyebrow in wry amusement. "Chelsea being a handful?"

"You could say that."

All at once she felt guilty for not being there with him. She'd agreed to help keep Chelsea at arm's length and that's what she had to do.

She swung her legs off the bed. "What's on the agenda for this afternoon?"

"Lunch and a lazy afternoon beside the pool."

Her head snapped toward him. "We're not swimming, are we? I didn't bring my swimsuit." She'd been thinking more along the lines of them all sitting around the drawing room, than prancing around the pool. She should have realized the pool would be more Chelsea and Todd's style.

"I'm sure one can be supplied."

"That's okay. I think I'll give the swimming a miss today." An imp of mischief reared its head. "Besides, I'm still feeling a little carsick from the long drive here."

He passed her an ironic look. "Then I won't swim, either. I don't want to encourage Chelsea."

Jenna nodded, relieved not to have to worry about

seeing Adam in his swimming briefs. It was just as well for Chelsea's sake, too. The other woman would eat him alive with her eyes. And Todd might notice.

"I'll just go freshen up." She went into the bathroom, having already unpacked. She'd left Adam's things for him. She wasn't any man's servant.

He had unpacked by the time she came out, and was sitting on the edge of the bed, waiting for her. She'd taken off her matching jacket before lying down, but now she wondered if she could leave it off altogether.

"Is this okay to wear?" she asked, indicating her sleeveless knit top, pants and strappy low-heeled sandals.

"You look lovely," he said huskily, pushing to his feet and coming toward her, an intent look in his eyes.

She put up her hand to stop him. "Don't even try it."

He stopped. "Try what?"

"Kissing me."

"I wasn't about to." He placed his hand on the small of her back and led her to the door. "We'd never get out of this bedroom otherwise."

They went downstairs together.

Jenna was relieved to see another six couples had been invited for the weekend. Everyone seemed very nice, and lunch in a shaded area by the pool ended up a chatty affair.

Chelsea and Todd were excellent hosts, though Jenna suspected Chelsea had brought in the other couples so no one would notice she had a thing for Adam. Jenna noticed. And a couple of times throughout the lunch, she even thought Todd was looking at his wife with an odd bleakness in his eyes. Yet he didn't appear to be watching Chelsea with Adam, and that was a relief. Something wasn't right between the other couple, but she couldn't put her finger on it.

Adam had been attentive at the Mayoral Ball, but now he took it to a new level. It wasn't exactly overkill but he made it clear to the others they were supposed to be lovers.

"Darling, here we go. Finish this off for me," he said, holding a fork up to her mouth with a small piece of Tasmanian salmon.

"No, I'd better not. I'm really quite full." She couldn't quite bring herself to use an endearment.

"But it's delicious, darling."

She could see he was enjoying paying her back for her earlier desertion. "I know. I had some already." She was aware of the others watching them.

"But I hate to waste it."

Then perhaps you could choke on it, she wanted to say, even as she gave in and let him place the fork in her mouth, somewhat surprised her gritted teeth didn't chew right through the metal.

"Good girl," he said as he withdrew the fork, his mockery for her eyes only, but also a sensuality in those depths that sent ripples under her skin.

He continued in the same vein with his dessert, then with the cheese and crackers. The hardest part for Jenna was *not* flinching whenever he touched her, and *not* blushing whenever he talked to her in that lowered voice. Crazily, after a while it gave her a strangely warm feeling having a man pay her attention like this. Lewis had been less than attentive at times.

After a suitable break, some of the others decided to go for a swim in the pool. Chelsea, with her fabulous body in front of Adam, teasingly tried to get him off the lounger to go change for a swim, while everyone laughed at her antics.

"No, I'm just too lazy today." He reached over to Jenna

lazing on the other lounger beside him and picked up her hand. "Jenna and I are just fine here."

Chelsea smiled and seemed to accept it, but Jenna thought she gave a rather childish flounce as she left to dive into the deep end of the pool. Jenna freed her hand from him as soon as she could without anyone noticing, but of course *he* noticed.

The afternoon whiled away. The staff put up large umbrellas to provide shade from the warmer autumn sunshine, and there was plenty of food and drink available. Jenna stuck to nonalcoholic drinks and she was pleased to see that Adam did, too. She had to say she enjoyed herself, and even he appeared to be relaxed…at least until Chelsea came to sit on a spare lounger near Adam and started vying for his attention in a way that could be construed as merely being sociable.

Jenna knew better.

And so did Adam, if the slight tension around his mouth was anything to go by.

So it was a relief when in late afternoon everyone got up to go and prepare for the dinner party. Of course, as Jenna followed Adam into their suite, she realized there were still some hours left before they had to go back downstairs. Suddenly, she was wary of how he might suggest they keep themselves occupied until then. Sharing that bed was out of the question.

He flopped onto the mattress and fell back against the pillows with a groan. "God, that woman exhausts me."

It dawned on her then that despite relaxing around the pool all afternoon, he hadn't really had a break from people since they'd left the city this morning. He'd been on the go all this time. "Take a nap," she suggested, feeling guilty because she'd been thinking only of herself.

He opened one eye. "You don't mind?"

"Not at all. I might go downstairs and see if I can find a book to read."

He opened two eyes. "You can't."

"Why?"

"We're supposed to be lovers. And I can tell you right now that I wouldn't be letting you out of my sight if that were true. We'd be making love."

Her stomach gave a quiver. "Then I'll go in the sitting room. There's some magazines on the table in there."

Something lurked in his eyes as he leaned up on his elbows. "You can join me here if you like."

"I don't like." She started toward the other room on legs that shook slightly.

"Pity." He collapsed on the pillows.

She glanced back at him as she left the room, seeing his eyes had closed. She was sure he was asleep as soon as the word was out of his mouth.

Instead of going straight to the magazines, she went out on the balcony and stood taking in the afternoon sun glinting on top of the hills. Her pulse took a while to settle, but eventually the superb view and sheer peace and quiet on this side of the house gave her a welcome respite after the nonstop chatter at the pool.

Whether it was the different surroundings or not, her hands began to itch and suddenly she was bursting with a new design for a pendant. If only she'd thought to bring her sketchbook, but she'd assumed she'd be too busy keeping Adam company.

Then she remembered the writing pad and pen she'd seen next to the magazines. She hurried back inside to the sitting room and sat at the small table, needing to draw while it was all so fresh and vivid in her mind.

How long she sat there she didn't know.

Not until Adam spoke behind her from the doorway. "What are you doing?"

She half twisted around to face him, sucking in a quick breath at the sight of his slightly tousled hair. He looked almost boyish...no, make that *playboy*-ish.

"I had an idea for a design."

His gaze went to the papers spread over the table. "Looks like you've drawn more than one," he said, coming into the sitting room and walking toward her.

She shrugged. "I guess I did sort of get carried away."

"Show me."

She looked down at the design she'd almost finished, then up at Adam again. "They're only rough," she said, remembering how uninterested Lewis had been in her designs.

"I'd still like to see them."

He seemed sincere, so she nodded. "Go ahead."

For the next minute he stood there studying them. She tried not to care what he'd think, but she knew she did. Finally, he looked at her with admiration. "These are really terrific."

Pleasure filled her. "You think so?" she said warmly.

"Absolutely. Roberto is very lucky to have you working for him."

"Thank you," she gushed, unable to stop herself, but it meant a great deal to hear him say that. Oh, she had full confidence in her designs, but this man had discerning tastes and she appreciated that.

Right then she caught an odd light in his eyes. She jumped to her feet. "I think I'll go take a shower." His eyes darkened and she saw his mouth open. "Alone," she preempted him.

His lips stretched into a smile. "I was merely going to say I would take a shower after you."

He might *say* that, but it wasn't what he'd been thinking, she knew, sending him a wry look before gathering up her designs and heading back into the bedroom.

Seeing the imprint of his body on the comforter made her steps falter. The intimacy of all this was quite overwhelming, and suddenly Stewart's money wasn't the issue between them. This was only about her and Adam. As fast as she could, she put her designs in her overnight case, then made for the shower.

When she came out of the bathroom ten minutes later, she was still feeling weird about sharing a room with a man she didn't know. Adam was sitting up against the pillows reading a magazine about yachting, but he lifted his head when the door opened. A thick bathrobe covered her from head to calf and she carried her day clothes, but he was actually looking at her bare face. She'd pulled her hair back in a ponytail and washed off her makeup, and he was assessing her in a way that pleased her. He didn't seem to be cringing, so she figured she didn't look too bad.

Going over to the chaise lounge, she began folding the clothes in her hands, giving herself something to do. "Chelsea told me there are some local dignitaries coming tonight," she said to cover up her nervousness.

He closed the magazine and put it aside. "I'm not surprised. Chelsea and Todd like to socialize."

"Well, I'm glad I brought a selection of clothes with me."

"I'm sure you managed to find something decent from..." He lifted a brow. "Now, where was that place? Vinnie's?"

She knew he was teasing her, and it turned her mouth dry. The temptation to smile at him and see where it would lead was almost irresistible.

Instead, she pursed her lips and played it cool. "I don't

always shop there, you know. I just wanted something special for the ball, that's all. I've got plenty of my own clothes for this sort of thing."

"You'd look fantastic in anything." He came off the mattress. "Or in nothing."

She stilled as he walked around the bed. His eyes were hot and she held her breath.

He kept walking…straight into the bathroom, and closed the door.

A pang of disappointment flooded her, embarrassed her. Damn him. He'd known what he was doing. He was toying with her, leaving her to wonder if he was ever going to kiss her again.

The sound of the shower being turned on released her feet from their fixed position. She hurried into the walk-in closet before he could come back out. Then as fast as she could, she dressed in a long black skirt and silky lilac top, applied her makeup in the vanity mirror and topped it all with a pair of dangling earrings she'd designed herself.

She was ready.

But she *wasn't* ready for the sight of him coming back into the bedroom with only a towel wrapped around his hips. The blood rushed in her ears as she swallowed hard and avoided his eyes, hurrying into the bathroom and closing the door. She definitely didn't need any blush for her cheeks after that, she decided, rubbing the steam from the mirror and staring at her heated reflection, then not leaving the room until she'd cooled down.

He was putting on his dark dinner jacket, dressing in front of her as if they were lovers, the action making her even more aware of them sharing a room together.

He turned to look at her and his eyes darkened. In three strides—one for each thump of her heartbeat—he was in front of her.

His head descended, and with the next beat of her heart she couldn't stop herself from opening her mouth to him. His tongue found hers, almost making her dissolve as he took her and teased, drawing her deep into a delicious well of sensation that was all about being with this man and no other. It was a kiss to die for.

Finally he let the pace slow, stopping and leaving her trembling. She swallowed the taste of him, then somehow managed to croak, "Let me guess. That's so people downstairs will think we're lovers."

"No, that one's for me."

Six

Downstairs, Adam watched Jenna from across the room as she talked to one of the couples they'd met this afternoon. By the darting glances she gave him and the slight flush under her skin, he knew she was aware he was watching her. Satisfaction filled him. After that kiss in the bedroom, he had no doubts she would be his lover before the night was over. He knew when a woman was on a losing battle. She might be able to say no to him, but she couldn't say no to herself.

"Adam, don't you think what William is saying is *so* interesting?" Chelsea enthused, drawing his attention back to her and the other man at her side.

He smiled politely at them both. "Of course." Chelsea had taken him away from Jenna on the pretext of introducing him to this bore of a person, but it had just been an excuse to separate them. God, he was so sick of this woman. If it wasn't for Todd he'd have no hesitation in setting her straight. He didn't like being held to ransom like this.

"William has quite a collection," Chelsea said.

"Does he, now?" Adam said, not the least interested in the other man's collection of butterflies. He'd prefer to collect women himself…and Jenna was one of them. And at least he'd set her free afterward, he mused.

Just then Adam saw the couple at Jenna's side go off to talk to someone else, leaving her standing alone. He was about to go to her when another man moved in, as if he'd been waiting for that exact opportunity, and she turned to him as though he was a lifeline in a sea of faces. Adam's hand tightened around his glass. That smile should be for *him*.

As fast as he could, he excused himself and moved to her side. "There you are, darling," he murmured, slipping his arm around her waist, feeling her give a start of surprise as he pulled her hip to hip. He sent the other man a definite look that she was *his*.

"Er…this is Franklin," Jenna said, looking wary.

"How do you do, Frank?"

The man's mouth pursed. "It's Franklin, actually."

"Franklin, then." Adam smiled briefly down at Jenna. "I see my lady has been keeping you company."

Franklin stiffened, clearly getting the picture. "We've just met." His eyes darted away. "If you'll excuse me, I see someone over there I know." He rushed off.

"Did you have to do that?" she whispered.

"Do what?"

"Scare him off like that. I might have wanted to get to know him better."

"Not on my watch, darling," he growled, taking a sip from his glass, his hand still holding her hip against him.

"Stop it. You don't have to call me that in private."

"But I'm only playing a part." Just as *she'd* been playing when she'd made her escape as soon as they'd arrived this morning. Of course, he'd made her pay at lunch when he'd offered her the food from his fork. Oh, that mouth of hers...

"You're going overboard with this stuff. I was merely talking to the guy and you're acting like a jealous lover."

He lifted a brow. "Isn't that the point?"

She blinked, then sighed. "Yes, of course."

Another couple came up to them then and the rest of the evening passed without incident. Adam refused to leave her side, not even when Chelsea tried to steal him away again. Neither woman had any chance of getting their wish.

Eventually the local guests began to depart, and Chelsea and Todd were kept busy seeing them to the front door. He saw Jenna look around at the six other couples staying here overnight, panic in her eyes, but it was a panic that was self-induced. He would never force a woman to do anything she didn't want to do. But if she *wanted* to do something...

He firmly took her by the arm. "Come on, darling. It's time we went to bed."

"Oh, but—"

"She's such a night owl at times," he joked to the others. "Good night, everyone." He led her from the room with a chorus of good-nights following them. It might be good-night for those people, but as far as he was concerned this was just the beginning.

Jenna wasn't sure how she managed it, but as Adam went to reach for her inside the bedroom, in her panic she sidestepped him to move a few feet away. "You can sleep over there," she said, jerking her head toward the chaise lounge near the window.

"No."

"You're *not* sleeping with me," she said, aware she was struggling to remain unaffected. He'd been stirring chords of longing in her all evening...all day—ever since she'd met him, actually.

"So you're not sleeping in the bed, then?" he mocked.

She watched him work his tie loose, and it was as if they were lovers coming home and getting ready for bed. As if they did this each night.

She swallowed hard. "You should be a gentleman and sleep on the lounge."

"Sorry. I like my comfort too much." He took off his jacket next and threw it over an upholstered chair. "Anyway, this bed's big enough for both of us."

"The *suite's* not big enough for both of us," she muttered, perhaps unwisely, she thought when she saw him moving toward her.

He took her by the arms. "You want me, Jenna," he said silkily. "I know you do. Let me show you how much."

Her stomach dipped. She wasn't sure why she was fighting this so hard. Perhaps because he expected her to cave in, and she wasn't going to let herself become one of his women. She'd fallen into bed with Lewis, and only ended up a number.

She lifted her chin. "I wouldn't appreciate it tomorrow."

With the speed of light the lines of his face turned rigid and he twisted toward the bathroom. "I'm going to brush my teeth, then I'm getting into bed. You sleep where you want."

The door closed and she stood there for a minute, her breathing unsteady, her knees shaky. She'd done the right thing, she told herself. This way at least she wasn't a statistic.

Knowing time was passing, she grabbed the comforter

and one of the pillows and dropped them on the chaise lounge. Then she quickly collected her makeup remover and hairbrush from the vanity and her night things from the dressing room. As soon as he came out of the bathroom, she went rushing past him, catching an unnerving glimpse of bare chest exposed by his undone shirt.

Her hands shook as she changed into her negligee and robe, then completed her toilette, but she held her head high as she came out of the bathroom. Damn him, he was sitting up in bed, his arms crossed behind his head. She almost stumbled when she saw the light from the bedside lamps spilling across his naked chest.

"Don't worry, I'm wearing the bottom half of my pajamas," he pointed out with a touch of sarcasm.

"Good."

Something in the air changed, and a deliberate pause hung in the room. "Not that I usually wear them. I generally prefer—"

"I never gave it a thought," she cut across him, not wanting to hear him say out loud that he generally wore nothing in bed. The picture was too vivid in her mind right now.

She placed her folded skirt and top on the chest of drawers, then went to the chaise lounge and began plumping up her pillow. She could feel his eyes on her.

"Don't you think you're being ridiculous?"

She placed the pillow back down and straightened. "No."

"You won't get a good night's sleep on that thing," he pointed out.

"And I will over there with you?" she scoffed, picking up the comforter next, intending to spread it over the lounge.

He smiled appreciatively, then it faded and his face took

on a serious note. "Look, we can put some pillows down the middle, if it'll ease your mind."

She halted, surprise rippling through her. "You would really do that?"

"Yes."

Then she made a face. "Ah, but can I trust you?"

"Of cour—"

Tap. Tap.

They both froze.

"Adam." Chelsea's voice came through the door. "I'm just checking that everything's okay."

A second passed, then Adam threw back the sheet on the other side of the bed. "Come and get in next to me," he whispered. "And take off that robe first."

Jenna heard the words but it was taking a moment to register. Get in bed with him? Take off her robe?

"Come on, hurry up," he said in a low voice, irritation crossing his face when she still didn't move. "Don't spoil it now," he rasped.

His words finally penetrated her mind. She dropped the comforter and did as he said, and soon he'd half dragged her across the sheets and into his arms before she could think or catch her breath.

"Adam?" Chelsea called out, louder this time, but not enough to disturb the other guests.

"Chelsea, everything's fine," he called out.

The door opened and she peeped around it. "I was just checking—" Her eyes flew to Jenna enfolded in the crook of his arm. There was no sign of Todd.

Feeling uncomfortable, Jenna tried to push herself away from Adam a little, but his arms tightened around her, keeping her firmly against his naked chest. She realized she was only making it look as if Chelsea had interrupted something.

A small flush rose in Chelsea's cheeks and she quickly looked away. Then her gaze rested on the pillow on the chaise lounge and the comforter on the floor next to it, and Jenna felt Adam tense beneath her.

Chelsea frowned. "You don't want the comforter?"

"No, we'll be warm enough," Jenna said quickly, and heard a rumble of laughter in Adam's throat. She looked up at him and saw the amusement on his face. Her cheeks heated up, playing right into his hands. She looked away again.

"Oh. Okay then." Chelsea still hesitated. "Well, let me know if you need anything."

"We will," Adam said.

There was an awkward silence.

"Good night, Chelsea," he said with more firmness this time.

"Good night." She closed the door and left them alone.

Jenna immediately went to push away, but his arms tightened. "Shh, stay there. She hasn't gone yet."

She stilled, waiting and listening. Half a minute passed. "Do you think she'll come back?"

"Who knows with Chelsea?"

"We should lock the door."

The words fell in a hush.

She felt the muscles of his chest flex beneath her palm and realized she was resting her hand on his bare skin. In fascination, she tilted her head back to find his eyes dark and deep and firmly on her. "Good idea," he murmured.

But he didn't move.

She wet her lips. "Er...the door," she reminded him, and waited for him to release her.

He stayed still. "Do you really want to sleep alone tonight, Jenna?"

Looking into his eyes, smelling his warm male scent and intently conscious of the side of his body against hers, it was hard to think coherently. "Um…I should."

"Should what?" He started to run his finger lazily down her bare arm. "Do you know how beautiful you are?"

Her heart started to race as she sensed something turn in the air. "Don't."

His finger drifted to a stop. "I want to make love to you."

Hearing him say it out loud in this tiny space between them made her gasp and had a red flag waving "Danger" in her mind. She had to get out of his arms before it was too late. She went to push back.

"Jenna?"

She stopped. His husky voice was working its way through her, draining her resistance. Who was she fooling? She didn't want him to let her go. She wanted this as much as he did.

The red flag turned white. She mentally let it drop in capitulation. "I want you, too," she heard herself whisper.

Surrender.

Something deep ignited in his eyes. "No regrets tomorrow?"

She shook her head. "No regrets tomorrow."

He paused a second longer. "Don't move," he said, and eased away from her to slide out from under the sheet.

He went to lock the door, then came back toward her in a pair of pajama pants that left nothing to her imagination. He was aroused, and it turned her into a mess of bones, especially when his hands went to the waistband, intent on taking the pants off.

"Not yet," she whispered, startling herself, aware she was suddenly afraid of losing total control. She'd never felt this way before with a man.

"I don't usually make love with my pants on," he teased.

Her throat felt blocked. "I'm not used to a...situation like this," she admitted. And she wasn't. She'd had a couple of lovers over the years, but they'd been men she'd thought she'd been in love with. And amazingly it hadn't felt as powerful as what she was feeling for this man—whom she didn't love.

His amusement disappeared. He wasn't teasing now. "Do you want me, Jenna?"

She took a deep breath. Did she really need to think about this? "Oh, yes, Adam. I do."

He turned the lamplight off. "Then when you're ready, *you* can take my pants off," he said in a low voice, and slid back into the bed beside her.

Jenna shuddered as Adam drew her into his arms. She was grateful he had turned off the lamp, more than thankful it left them in a privacy of moonlight. They could see each other, but it was her eyes she wanted to hide from him as much as possible. In the dark he would not be able to see into their depths.

Of course, concealing her body's reactions from him was impossible—nor did she want to—but that was all she wanted him to see. If he discovered that he affected her more with one touch of his finger, one crook of his smile, than any man had ever done before him, he might just use that against her when it came time to resolve their family issues. She couldn't allow him that.

Lord, she was thinking too much, she decided, gladly welcoming his kiss, pushing all thought to the back of her mind. His mouth enticed her to open her lips fully, and she slid into a moan as his tongue swept in...and swept her breath away, the effect no less than searing.

Then he took his time playing with her tongue, but soon he must have needed air, too. He broke off the kiss and sucked in a solid gasp of oxygen before grazing along the top of her shoulder, his fingers pushing the thin strap of her negligee aside, letting it fall partway down her arm, baring her skin for his warm lips. He did the same to the other side, then moved back to gaze at the sight of her bare shoulders lashed by the silk material.

He groaned and kissed her again, his hand working its way down to her hip, sensually caressing every inch he touched through her nightgown. The blood in her veins turned syrupy and pooled low in her belly. Her nipples ached for him to lower his head and suck their throbbing tips, and she eagerly awaited his mouth on her breasts. Instead, he got on his knees and lifted the hem of her nightgown, sliding the silky fabric up and over her head, leaving her only in her panties. His gaze glittered through the moonlight, burning a path over every single inch of her. The impact made her head whirl.

And then he was running his palms over her breasts in an outward circular motion, making her take a shaky breath as he targeted her sensitized nipples. Her head pressed back on the pillows as she let him have his way for long, glorious moments, his touch wonderful.

Suddenly, she wanted to see him, too. And to touch him. Normally, she wouldn't feel so forward. She'd never had such a strong urge to reach out for a man…to know every inch of him…. It should be scaring the hell out of her, but she couldn't think past the moment. She pushed herself to her knees, bringing them face-to-face.

She was first to reach out, surprised a little that he'd let her take the lead. Her palms tingled as she moved over his hot, dampening chest, her fingers prickling at the heavy

Send For
2 FREE BOOKS
Today!

I accept your offer!

Please send me two
free Silhouette Desire®
novels and two mystery
gifts (gifts worth about $10).
I understand that these books
are completely free—even
the shipping and handling will
be paid—and I am under no
obligation to purchase anything, ever,
as explained on the back of this card.

About how many NEW paperback fiction books have you purchased in the past 3 months?

❏ 0-2   ❏ 3-6   ❏ 7 or more
E7WH   E7WT   E7W5

225/326 SDL

Please Print

FIRST NAME

LAST NAME

ADDRESS

APT.#   CITY

STATE/PROV.   ZIP/POSTAL CODE

Visit us online at
www.ReaderService.com

◀ Detach card and mail today. No stamp needed. ◀

S-D-07/10

beat of his heart beneath the smooth skin and wisps of masculine hair.

"You surprise me," he said gruffly, as her hands advanced over his rib cage. "I thought you might be shy."

She stroked his firm stomach. "You thought wrong."

A challenge flew from his eyes. "Wrong?" He reached out and slid a finger down under her panties with exact precision, through her curls, parting her. She almost came undone when he began a delicate manipulation, her head falling back as he continued the action, her bended knees weakening. She wasn't sure how long they would hold her up.

He laughed low in his throat. "No, I don't think I was wrong at all."

From somewhere she found the strength to straighten up. This had suddenly become a game of who would succumb first. Oh, she knew she couldn't win—not the way he was making her feel—but she'd give it a damn good try....

"Then you'd better think again," she murmured, deliberately slipping her fingers under the waistband of his pajamas, slowly pushing them down to his knees. She took in the sight of his manly hips, the arrow of curly hair, his shaft hard and fully erect, ready to take, to conquer and to totally consume her.

Reaching out, she slid her hand around his thickened length, then proceeded to stroke him. "Oh, yes, dead wrong."

Without warning, he flipped her backward onto the mattress.

Her eyes widened. "Hey, that's not fair."

"Tell it to someone who cares," he drawled.

Then he shed his pajamas, and her panties soon disappeared. His kisses became deeper and hungrier as she returned each one. He ran his hands over her, touching places that came close again to making her lose her head. Hot on her trail.

"Adam, please," she begged, when he rubbed himself between her thighs, then moved away, leaving her wanting. "I need you."

"Shh." He reached over to the night table.

She turned her head on the pillow and watched him take a condom from his wallet. "You knew I'd sleep with you?" she said half to herself, but she wasn't angry with him. She couldn't be. She just wanted him inside her.

"I was hoping." He sheathed himself before slowly entering her, and then he began the heated thrust of his body. It was slow, it was deliberate, and it sent shock waves of sensation pulsing through her veins.

And when she finally did lose her head, Adam did too, locking them together on an unstoppable journey until they exploded their release.

Seven

The next morning Adam lay in bed beside Jenna, watching her sleep in his arms. It amazed him that he wanted her again so soon with so much hunger. Sure, he was a man with a healthy sexual appetite, but when he woke in the morning with a woman in his bed it always felt like he was dining on a light breakfast. Of course, more often than not he usually *wanted* something light anyway.

But with Jenna, it was as if he was being offered a wholesome breakfast…as if it filled him…completed him even…as if she satisfied something substantial in him.

Last time he'd felt like that had been with Maddie.

Bloody hell!

He dropped his eyelids again, pushing all thoughts of his late wife to the back of his mind. This wasn't the time or place to be thinking about the woman who had introduced him to love.

When he opened his eyes again sometime later, Jenna was looking at him. "I see you're not an early riser."

He gave a low chuckle and pushed himself forward against her. "I wouldn't say that."

She blushed. "You know what I mean."

"No, show me."

Her hand touched him and he was instantly lost. Afterward they showered together, made love again, then dressed and headed downstairs.

Adam had to admit he was surprised by her. Other women wanted to talk and decipher everything, sometimes wanting a declaration of love or commitment, yet Jenna seemed to be happy to just be with him.

And when they walked into the breakfast room to find Todd and Chelsea there alone, Jenna didn't gloat, like the other women he knew would gloat at being made his lover. In a way he wished she would, rather than being sensitive to Chelsea's feelings. It was what they were here for after all.

Yet how could he fault Jenna when her actions were showing him a depth of character he was only now beginning to appreciate?

"Good morning," he said, holding a chair out for Jenna but smiling at Todd and Chelsea. For a moment the other couple sat there in a kind of stony silence, making him suddenly aware of the tension in the air.

Then Todd put on a forced smile. "Good morning. Did you both sleep well?"

Adam sat down next to Jenna, but he watched Todd. "Yes. What about you two?"

Todd's smile was tight. "Terrific. This country air has me sleeping like a log."

"I'm glad someone did, then," Chelsea snapped, much to Adam's surprise. He felt Jenna startle, too.

"Chels…" Todd said in a warning tone.

For a second Chelsea looked as if she would snap at him

again, but then she seemed to realize she had an audience. She pulled a face. "Sorry about that. I've got the beginnings of a headache."

Adam remembered what Todd had said about Chelsea's female problems, but her excuse just now didn't gel. It had been too glib.

"Perhaps you should go lie down," Jenna said sympathetically.

Antagonism flared in Chelsea's eyes, then banked, and she put on a bright smile for everyone to see. "No, I'll be fine."

At that point Adam suspected that Chelsea's ill health was more likely due to her jealousy over seeing him and Jenna in bed together last night. For a brief second he wondered if he hadn't unwittingly dumped Jenna in the middle of something impossible, but then he remembered she was tough. If Jenna could handle *him,* she could handle Chelsea.

The arrival of the other guests in the breakfast room brought a flurry of chatter. Chelsea seemed to go into overdrive, her eyes extra bright as she turned into the perfect hostess. It didn't disguise the hint of hostility in the air, though after watching her send one or two dark glances at her husband, Adam had to wonder if this was more about Todd than not.

"So this morning we have a lot of activities to get through," Chelsea said now. "There's tennis, horseback riding and swimming to choose from, or you can choose all three—if you're game," she joked, with a wink. "And after lunch I've arranged for a tour of a local winery. I can guarantee you'll love it," she enthused just a little bit too shrilly.

Adam saw Jenna dart a look at him, and he knew

instantly what she was thinking. He agreed. He didn't want to stay any longer, either.

"I'm afraid we can't stay, Chelsea," he said, placing his napkin on the table. "Jenna and I both have to get back to the city for another commitment that's come to light."

"But you can't!"

He stiffened in anger. No one told him what he could or couldn't do, especially not someone who had no claim to his time.

Chelsea seemed to notice she'd made a mistake, but that didn't quite stop her. "Surely you can stay, Adam," she said in a pleading tone. "Please say you will."

Her comment irritated the hell out of him. It would have irritated him whether he and Jenna were lovers or not, but she appeared to be ignoring Jenna, and that was the height of bad manners. "Sorry," he said, not sorry at all.

"But—"

Todd pushed to his feet then, sending his wife a hard look before turning to their guests. "How about we all go change into something more casual so that we can start the activities? Chelsea has arranged a selection of sports gear for anyone who may need it." He glanced at Adam and smiled. "Let me know when you and Jenna are ready to leave, Adam," he said, silently indicating he had no problem with their early departure. "I'll see you off."

Adam nodded, then cupped Jenna's elbow and pushed both of them to their feet. "I will. Thanks. We won't be too long." He led Jenna out of the room, but another couple followed and conversed with them as they went up the stairs.

In the bedroom he was still disgusted by Chelsea's actions. "Let's get our stuff together," he said, striding away.

A couple of seconds passed, then she said, "Chelsea was upset."

He turned at the entrance to the walk-in closet and saw she hadn't moved. "It's because she knew we'd made love last night."

Jenna blushed a little, even as she looked baffled. "Didn't she already believe we were lovers?"

"Yes, but seeing us in bed together must have finally hit home."

She nodded, then a sigh escaped. "I'm glad we're leaving soon."

"So am I," he said pointedly, growing fascinated by her pink cheeks. Thoughts of Chelsea faded from his mind.

As if trying to ignore her own embarrassment, Jenna tilted her head. "Do you really have a commitment in the city?"

This woman was enthralling. "Yes." Casually he leaned against the doorjamb, slowing things down for a few moments. "I'm committed to making love to you all afternoon."

Her eyes flared with pleasure. "I see."

He loved the little pulse that started throbbing at her neck. If he hurried back to her, he could put his lips against it…no, then he wouldn't want to stop. He'd want to pull her into his arms and make love to her again.

"Come on," he said brusquely, pushing himself away from the wooden frame. "Let's pack our things and get out of here."

Todd was waiting at the bottom of the stairs when they came down. "Chelsea asked me to give you her apologies. She and some of the others have gone to the stables."

Adam was relieved not to be seeing her again so soon. "That's fine, Todd. Please give her our thanks."

Jenna smiled. "It's been a lovely weekend. I've really enjoyed it."

"I'm glad." Todd's expression seemed strained. "And I'm sorry about things this morning."

Adam looked at his friend with concern. "Is everything okay between you and Chelsea?"

Todd waved a dismissive hand. "Don't take any notice of Chels. She's just on edge with…everything."

Adam wanted to ask if the "everything" involved *him*, only he couldn't. If he was responsible for Chelsea's bad mood, he certainly didn't want Todd to know it.

Just then, two of the male guests came out of the drawing room and saw them standing in the entrance, preparing to leave.

"Hey, there's the man who'll remember," one of the men said, coming toward them. "Adam, what was the name of the guy your father had convicted of fraud? It was about five years ago. Burke something or other…"

Adam froze, then he said tightly, "Milton Burke."

"Oh, yeah, that's the guy's name. He ended up doing a couple of years in prison, didn't he?" The guest didn't wait for an answer. "Yeah, old Milt was a professional con man. He—"

"We're leaving," Adam cut across him, not caring if he appeared rude. Taking Jenna by the arm, he turned away and strode out the front door of the mansion to where his car was waiting. Their overnight bags had already been put in the trunk, and after a brief farewell to Todd, he drove off the estate.

"Er…are you okay, Adam?" Jenna asked once they were on the road.

He glanced at her. "Never better," he quipped.

After that he concentrated on the driving, making it clear he didn't want to talk. He wasn't angry with her, just with the way things were. The mention of money and fraud back there had called to mind what stood between him and this woman who was now his lover. Stewart Branson was back between them again like a brick wall, though truth be told that wall had never really fallen down.

Dammit, between Jenna's brother and Todd's wife, life was getting far too complicated.

And he didn't like it one bit.

By the time they reached the city just after lunch, Jenna was trying not to worry. Adam had been remote from the minute the mention was made of the guy who'd gone to prison for fraud. It was a powerful reminder that the Roth family was far from lenient if they were wronged.

Not that Stewart had done anything wrong. Far from it. *He* was the one wronged.

But with Adam so quiet beside her now, she couldn't stop from worrying about *their* relationship. Was he having misgivings because they were back in town? Had it merely been the country air? A mistake on his part?

"Do you regret making love to me, Adam?" she had to ask as soon as they stepped inside her apartment.

"Time's too short for regrets," he muttered, then swung her up in his arms and headed for the bedroom. She wasn't exactly sure why his words didn't thrill her, but she was soon preoccupied enough not to think about it just then.

He left late afternoon with the promise to call.

After he'd gone, Jenna wondered about the state of their relationship. They hadn't spoken about being faithful to each other, but would he be committed to her while their affair lasted? She had to remember Adam had no ties to her. He owed her no loyalty—except the loyalty of a lover. To her, that was everything. To him, it might not be.

No, she had to believe that he *would* remain faithful. He wasn't like Lewis. Already she knew he had more integrity in his little finger than Lewis had from head to toe. She only had to see how Adam *hadn't* slept with his best friend's wife. It was admirable.

And yet—in spite of knowing that Adam would treat her well—she couldn't help but admit something was bothering her. She was now another man's mistress.

Again.

At least with Lewis she'd thought she loved him and that they had a future together. She had no long-term future with Adam. Their divided loyalties ensured it would never work between them anyway.

And that prompted the question—why had she changed her resolve and become Adam's lover? She'd been so determined not to get involved, yet now in one brief overnight trip she'd slept with him. She could only think those very loyalties that stood between them showed a man who put himself second when it came to the people he cared about. She found that very appealing, especially in a successful businessman whose spare time was limited.

So here she was.

A mistress.

Again.

Perhaps she should just enjoy being his mistress while she could—even if it didn't change the facts.

Later that evening Jenna's telephone rang and she raced to pick it up, hoping it was Adam. "Hello," she said, her heart thumping.

No answer.

She blinked, then listened hard, but there was only silence. "Hello?" she repeated, thinking it could be a wrong number and the other person had been caught off balance.

More silence.

She began to feel uneasy now. "Who is this?"

Another couple of seconds passed, then she thought she heard a woman's sigh just before the person quietly ended the call.

Jenna shivered with apprehension as she replaced the handset. If it *had* been a wrong number, then surely the person would have simply hung up straight away. If it had been family or friends, then…

Chelsea!

She wasn't sure how she knew it was the other woman. It just…fit. It hadn't been a threatening silence, more disconcerting. Could Chelsea have been checking to see if Adam was still with her? And did that mean Chelsea had tried Adam's apartment and received no answer? He was probably catching up on work and didn't want to be interrupted.

And how the heck had Chelsea gotten her phone number anyway? She grimaced. It wasn't really surprising, considering who the other woman was.

The question for Jenna was whether she should tell Adam about this. If she did he might put his relationship with Todd at risk, when there was no proof it had been Chelsea at all. It would be best to wait and see how things panned out first.

Half an hour later, the phone rang again. Jenna cautiously answered, thankful this time it was her mother, and pushed aside her disappointment that it wasn't Adam.

Joyce Branson was her usual cheery self, talking about the championship game of tennis that was coming up and whining a little about Jenna's father being home and in the way now that he was retired. She didn't ask anything about Adam.

Then her mother mentioned how she'd seen Vicki and the children, but said how she was still worried about Stewart being so far away from his family. That refreshed Jenna's worry. It was amazing how on the surface everything seemed normal—even if it wasn't. It pained her to keep secrets from her parents.

At work the following morning she found herself checking her cell phone in case Adam called. Constantly. There were no calls, but she was eternally grateful that Marco didn't make an appearance. She didn't think she could have stood the questions she'd have to field about her and Adam's relationship.

Normally, she loved her job, but the day dragged and she was grateful to arrive home, eager to see if Adam called that evening. She tried to persuade herself that he probably wouldn't for a few days, and when the phone didn't ring over the next few hours she had to accept it. He had other priorities, she told herself, but to no avail. Her heart was just about convinced she'd hear nothing, when the doorbell rang around eight.

It was Adam.

His eyes drank her up as he stepped inside and kicked the door shut. Without a word, he caught hold of her hips and brought them flush up against him, his hardened body making her gasp. It was clear he'd been wanting her before he'd even reached her door. The thought of it made her feel more feminine than ever before.

Then he pressed her back against the wall and kissed her, and he kept right on kissing her until her toes curled in her shoes and her knees threatened to buckle. He stopped for a breath, but not for long. His fingers went on the move, working open her blouse, undoing her trousers.

"Why can't I get enough of you?" he murmured, with a darkening look of desire in his eyes, his lips creating havoc as he bent his head and began to lavish each nipple through her lacy bra. Then he kissed down her stomach…farther down until his fingers lowered the front of her panties so he could access her with his mouth…to where she was more than ready for him.

She held his head to her while he pleasured her, until tremors started to shake her body and her breath came as fast as the upwelling explosion.

After she climaxed, he stepped her out of her panties and swept her up in his arms, carrying her over to the couch, where he sat her down. With her heart in her throat and barely able to catch her breath, Jenna watched as he stood there and undid his trousers in front of her. Her hand tingled to—

"Not this time," he muttered, preempting her touching him as he ripped the wrapper from a condom and sheathed himself. Then he sat next to her, pulled her on top of his hard length and entered her.

"Adam!" she cried out as he groaned and filled her with all that he was. She grew hot. Instinctively, she lifted herself an inch…then slid down on him. She did it again and he caught her by the hips, holding her so that she could easily fall into a rhythm that was beautifully exquisite. Their eyes on each other, they soon climaxed together.

"Oh, my God," she muttered when they'd finished and their foreheads were resting against each other while they caught their breath. Then she dragged in some air and lifted her head away from his. "Is it always like this?" she whispered, half in wonder, but regretting it the instant the words were out of her mouth. "No, don't answer that." She didn't want to hear his response. To him, this was a regular occurrence.

Adam put his hand under her chin and made her look him in the eyes. "No, it isn't always like this."

Her heart tilted sideways. "Oh."

As if he'd said enough, his face turned blank and he lifted her off him and went into the bathroom. She sat there for a moment, telling herself she wouldn't be normal if she didn't feel thrilled at his words.

And yet as she tidied her clothes, she was concerned. In the long run it would have been better if there hadn't been this intense attraction between them. In the long run she'd have to survive without him…without *this,* she decided, fully aware she'd never be able to look at her couch again without thinking of the two of them here. Suddenly, she felt an odd pain at the thought. Maybe after this was over she'd get a new couch. Hell, she might even sell this apartment and buy a new one. Start afresh. She had the feeling she might need to get totally away from memories of Adam.

"Have you eaten?" she asked, when he came back.

He sent her a dry look. "Yes."

"I'm talking about dinner."

"So am I," he teased, then nodded. "Yes, I've eaten. I had a business dinner."

She was surprised. "You finished early."

"I wanted to see you."

He had? Why? Had he discovered she'd been telling the truth about the money? Why else would he come here after a long day at work? She swallowed. And why didn't she feel happier than she did? She should be ecstatic for Stewart's sake.

"Um…about anything important?" she asked, trying to sound idle.

"Yes. I needed to make love to you." He pulled her up close. "And I did." Then he kissed her briefly. "I have to go. I have some work to finish up tonight for an early morning meeting."

Relief ribboned through her that the money clearly wasn't his main concern right now, then she felt bad for her family's sake. She couldn't be selfish enough to take her happiness at their cost.

So it was a good thing that Adam wasn't staying the night, she told herself as she walked him to the door. He was respecting her space as she respected his. It kept the lines divided.

"I'll call you."

She nodded, but as she closed her door she wondered if this was how their relationship was supposed to work from now until their time was up. Was she to wait around for his call all the time—at his whim—like a mistress who dropped everything for his pleasure and had no life of her own?

Something inside her flattened at the thought.

Over the next few evenings the same thing happened. Adam never promised to see her, but invariably he'd turn up around eight and make love to her. They even made it to her bedroom most of the time and she'd hope he would stay the night, but after a while he would take himself home. It made her think even harder. Was he actually giving her some space?

Or himself?

Eight

Adam hadn't intended to visit Jenna again so soon, but somehow on Thursday evening he found himself heading for her apartment. Every night this week he'd aimed to go straight home after work, only it hadn't quite worked out that way.

It was disconcerting to realize he'd never physically wanted a woman so much as he did Jenna. The need to be inside her thickened his blood and stirred his pulse. He'd constantly had to put thoughts of her aside throughout the day. He'd be in the middle of a meeting and picture her gasping her climax. Or he'd be reading a report and his mind would wander to untying her silky bathrobe and kissing her all over.

Tonight on his arrival he did exactly that. She tasted good. She felt good. And she was damn good in bed. But as he was dressing to go home, he suddenly felt as if he should be offering her more—though more than what he wasn't sure.

"Can you make dinner tomorrow night?" he heard himself ask.

One elegant eyebrow rose as she slipped into her bathrobe. "Another function?"

"No. It'll just be the two of us."

"Alone?"

He had to smile. "The two of us alone, yes. Well, as alone as we can get in a restaurant."

It took her a moment to think about it. "So this isn't for Chelsea and Todd's benefit, then?"

"No." He hadn't heard from the other couple since last weekend, and right now he didn't give a damn.

Jenna flashed him a smile. "That would be lovely."

That gorgeous smile rocked something inside him, and suddenly he was scrambling to put them back on a physical relationship. "Bring an overnight bag."

"A...bag?"

"You'll be spending the night at my place."

She looked pleased, but as he drove home he was glad she didn't know his thoughts. Perhaps he'd made a mistake in narrowing it all down to just the two of them. He didn't want her getting the idea that anything further could develop...and yet he didn't have the heart to cancel. Besides, it was only a matter of time before their relationship began to wane anyway.

And then there was the money issue between them.

It was just as well he had a meeting arranged with the forensic accountant. The guy was still checking it out, and so far there was nothing to report, but Adam still wanted an update in person first thing Monday.

And that prompted the question—what if the money couldn't be found?

* * *

The following evening Jenna was thrilled to be dining alone with Adam—until Lewis Carter showed up with his latest girlfriend on his arm as they were finishing their dinner. She saw him a split second too late.

"Jenna?" He stopped as he passed by their table.

She pasted on a smile, more aware of Adam's interest than she wanted to be. "Yes. How are you, Lewis?" Not that she cared one way or the other.

Lewis's eyes darted to Adam, and he gave a nod of recognition before returning to her. "Totally heartbroken you didn't return my calls."

He made it sound as if she'd been the one at fault, and not the other way around. Ooh, how typical of the man! It would serve him right if she reminded him of his unfaithfulness.

And revenge was sweet….

She reached across the table and slid her hand over the top of Adam's, giving the dreamiest smile she could muster before looking up at Lewis. "Now you can see why."

There was a moment when Lewis's smile stretched like a piece of elastic. Then he bounced right back. "You're still quick off the mark, Jenna, my love."

"And you're still—" *a jerk* "—the same."

Lewis's date started to fidget from lack of attention. "Honey, can we go sit down? I'm starving."

He laughed and winked at them. "She has quite the appetite."

With a bad taste in her mouth Jenna watched them walk away.

"So you dated Lewis Carter."

"Don't remind me," she muttered, turning back to Adam, a little surprised he hadn't already investigated her previous relationships, especially considering her claim about Stewart. "Obviously you know him. He recognized you, too."

"We've met a couple of times."

Her lips twisted. "Lucky you."

Adam looked amused. "At least he appreciates your wit."

"It's about the only thing he did appreciate."

His amusement faded. "What happened?"

She picked up her glass of wine and took a sip before speaking. Better to say it and get it out in the open. She had nothing to hide. "I met Lewis when we both backed out of our parking spaces at a shopping center one day. There wasn't a lot of damage, but he insisted on taking me for a drink to calm my nerves. We exchanged names and addresses for our insurance companies and—" she gave a wry shrug "—it went from there."

"How long were you his girlfriend?"

"About six months."

"I'm surprised Carter could remain faithful for that long."

"He didn't. I thought he was getting serious, but he was *serious* only about cheating on me."

His gaze intensified on her. "I would never cheat on you, Jenna."

"Thank you," she murmured, meaning it.

But a second later she couldn't help thinking it would be easy for him to remain faithful for the short period of time they had left together. As quickly, she chastised herself. That wasn't fair of her. She'd already decided Adam wasn't like Lewis.

He studied her some more before speaking again. "Carter didn't like your designs, did he?"

Her eyes widened. "How did you know that?"

"You were self-conscious about showing me your

drawings back at the Grampians. It was almost as if you expected me to criticize them."

She was touched by his perception. "I'm glad you didn't," she said softly.

His eyes stayed on her for a few beats, the blue irises darkening with desire before he pushed back his chair and held out his hand. "Let's go."

She had no argument with that. She was more than ready to concentrate on her and Adam again—and more than ready to forget Lewis Carter.

Adam took her back to his apartment, and they made love over and over during the night—as if they hadn't seen each other all week—as if they hadn't touched each other at all in that time. Lewis was far from her mind and yet she knew he was partly responsible for the intensity of their lovemaking. Seeing her ex-lover again reminded her that what she had with Adam was very special. And Lewis would hate to know that.

They slept until late Saturday morning, when Adam groaned and rolled out of bed. "I've got to go. I've got a meeting with a business acquaintance in half an hour."

Jenna lay on the pillow, sleepily distracted by the sight of his naked torso. "You're working today? It's Saturday."

He strode toward the bathroom. "It was supposed to be on Monday, but something came up and now the guy's going to be out of town then." He stopped to look at her with an odd smile she couldn't decipher. "You stay here and I'll be back in a couple of hours."

Jenna dozed lightly while Adam showered and dressed, but after he left, she pushed herself out of bed and headed for the shower, too.

She was enjoying her second cup of coffee and thinking about making herself a late lunch when the concierge called up to say that Adam's mother was here to see him. She held her breath. Obviously the man had only started his shift recently, or he would have known that Adam had left earlier.

Her breath started up again as she tried to think. What was the protocol here? Would Adam want his current lover to meet his mother? Shouldn't she just say Adam wasn't home and let Laura Roth come back later?

Then she remembered.

Liam Roth.

Didn't *she* want to meet the mother of the man who had cheated her brother? "Please tell her to come up," she said, curiosity getting the better of her.

Then she checked herself in the mirror to make sure she looked presentable before going over to wait at the private elevator. Soon the doors were sliding open and an elegant woman stepped out. Jenna hesitated a moment, forgetting the money issues, taken slightly aback to be greeting such a prominent person.

And sleeping with her middle son.

In the end, Adam's mother spoke first. "Hello, I'm Laura Roth," she said with a warm smile, offering a manicured hand.

Jenna was surprised by her warmth. She pulled herself together enough to shake her hand, though she rather felt like she should curtsy. It was natural to be formal with such a woman. "Hello, Mrs. Roth."

"Call me Laura."

Jenna didn't think she could do that. "Please, come right in," she said politely, and led the way farther into the living room. She should dislike the woman for what Liam had done to the Bransons, only she wasn't getting that feeling. "I wasn't sure whether to ask you to come up or not. Adam's gone out, you see. He had to meet a business acquaintance."

"On a Saturday?" His mother tutted. "I shouldn't be surprised."

Jenna noticed a curious light at the back of the other woman's eyes, but at least his mother was too well-bred to ask outright if she was her son's mistress. "He'll be back soon if you want to wait."

Laura shook her head. "I can't. I'm off to lunch with a friend in the city, and I just thought I'd stop in and see Adam as I was passing. I wanted to ask him to pick up his cousin when he comes to lunch tomorrow. Logan's car is in the shop getting a minor repair and I told him not to bother about using one of our drivers. It's not out of Adam's way."

She nodded. "I'll make sure he gets the message."

"Thank you."

Just then, the elevator pinged open and Adam strode in wearing a frown. "Mum, you should have let me know you were coming," he scolded as he kissed his mother's cheek.

"That's okay, darling. Jenna's been looking after me."

"Has she, now?" Adam turned to look at Jenna, a warning in his eyes, telling her she'd better not say anything about Liam or Stewart. Jenna didn't want to use the situation for her own benefit, but remembering her brother and his wife and how close they were to losing their home, she defiantly lifted her chin a little at Adam.

He noticed.

"I have to go," Laura said after glancing at her slim gold watch. "I have a lunch date."

Adam's gaze returned to his mother. "With Dad?"

Laura smiled as she headed for the elevator. "No, with Della." She pressed the button, then turned around. "Jenna, you should come to lunch tomorrow with Adam. Now that Dominic and Cassandra are back from their second honeymoon, we're having a family get-together."

Jenna darted a look at Adam and saw the alarm in his eyes. "Laura, thank you, but I don't want to intrude."

"Do you have a previous engagement?"

"No, but—"

"Then I insist." She stepped into the elevator. "See you both tomorrow. Don't forgot to collect Logan, darling."

The doors slid closed.

Silence echoed through the apartment.

Jenna stared at Adam. She could see he wasn't pleased. "I'm sorry. I'll come up with an excuse and you can give my apologies."

"No."

Her forehead crinkled. "But I thought—"

"We're going." His tone brooked no argument.

She considered that. He definitely didn't want her near his parents, yet he was making her go?

"Aren't you worried I'll say something about the money?" It would be the perfect time to take advantage of being near his family, especially his older brother and his wife. After all, Cassandra had been married to Liam before she'd married Dominic. She would be the one who could know something.

"No, I'm not worried. I can easily repay the favor, or have you forgotten that?"

Her stomach clenched. When it came down to it, he didn't trust her. And it stunned her to think that it should even matter. They were lovers in one aspect of their lives, but enemies in another. "I know exactly where things stand, Adam."

As if he suspected more than she was saying, his glance sharpened. "I'm thinking this will work out with Chelsea.

If she hears I took you home to meet my parents, she might finally give up trying."

So that was why he'd agreed. She should have realized. "Or it might make her even more desperate to get your attention," she pointed out. "Chelsea's a very determined woman. Don't underestimate her."

"I don't underestimate any woman."

Her chest felt tight. "There you go, then," she said, turning away to go into the kitchen and fix them a light lunch, giving herself something to do.

After that, Adam was quiet as they sat on the balcony and ate in the sunshine. He wasn't as relaxed as he'd been previously. It wasn't that he was rude, but there was a withdrawal in the air that suddenly made her ache inside.

Jenna wasn't comfortable staying the rest of the day, and when she made an excuse about needing to go and work on a design, she caught a glint of relief in his eyes. She pretended not to notice as he offered to get his driver to take her home.

"No, I'll catch a cab."

"But—"

"You don't need to see me home," she said firmly, knowing she had to get out of here and away from him. Her company wasn't wanted right now and she could feel it all the way through her bones.

He took a long moment to nod. "I'll collect you tomorrow around noon."

She shot him a quick look. "I'm sorry if it's making things awkward for you. I really could cancel, you know. Just this once we could forget all about Chelsea."

A muscle ticked in his cheek. "No, my mother invited you, Jenna. You have to go, whether we like it or not. We may as well use the situation."

It wasn't the answer she wanted to hear and she turned

away to collect her things, disheartened. She hadn't taken a step when he pulled her up close and kissed her. At least he still wanted her physically.

But in the cab home she suspected that somehow she'd just crossed her own personal line. Adam had chosen her because he'd trusted she wouldn't get emotionally involved with him. Too late she realized she might already have done exactly that.

Adam stood at Liam's bedroom window at his parents' mansion and looked down on the terrace below where his family sat around a poolside table after Sunday lunch. There was much teasing and joking today. It was so damn good hearing laughter in this house again.

It was clear to everyone now that Dominic and Cassandra were meant to be together. Adam was convinced Liam had known it when he'd secretly asked Dominic to supply sperm to give her a baby. Poor Dominic had suffered a great deal because of that, knowing he had fathered a child he'd been unable to acknowledge until after Liam had died. But now everything was fine and out in the open, and Adam knew that Liam would be happy up there in heaven with the way things had turned out. For Dominic anyway. For himself, he was wondering what the hell Liam had dragged him into.

"Adam, what are you doing in here?"

Startled, he turned around, glad of a respite from his thoughts. "Nothing, Mum. I just had the urge to come up here, that's all."

His mother's face softened as she took a few steps inside the bedroom. "You miss your brother, don't you? We all do, darling."

He searched her face. "Are *you* okay?" he asked with concern. "It hasn't been that long. Not really."

"Three months. And I miss him with an ache that leaves

a hole in my heart, but I think I'm finally accepting that he's gone." She eased into a smile. "I have so much to be thankful for."

He watched her. She was right, yet his heart still ached for her. To lose a child...

"And you, darling?" she said gently. "This week is going to be hard on you."

His chest tightened. "You remembered."

"Of course. Maddie's death left a big hole in all our hearts, but none more than yours. We wouldn't forget her, not on the fifth anniversary of her passing, not even on the twenty-fifth anniversary. She's in our hearts, darling."

"Thanks, Mum," he said gruffly. He was aware his mother didn't know the full story, and he was glad she'd been spared. For his mother to know she had lost an unborn grandchild as well as a beloved daughter-in-law wasn't something he'd ever let her discover. He'd keep that from her forever.

"And now you have Jenna," she said gently.

His head went back. "Why do you say that?"

"I like this one. I think she's a keeper."

He didn't want to get into this discussion. He didn't need this right now. Yet he couldn't stop himself from asking, "Why?"

"She's a brunette."

He raised an eyebrow. "So?"

"You always go out with blondes." She hesitated. "Ever since Maddie, that is."

He stiffened. He hadn't realized. "Don't make the mistake of thinking there's more than there is. Jenna and I aren't serious. Everything else is a mere coincidence."

"Darling, you—"

"Mum, don't try and marry me off," he snapped, then saw her flinch. He winced. "Sorry, I don't mean to sound harsh, but I don't intend to marry again. Not for a long time, if ever. I'm happy with my life these days. I intend to keep it that way."

She stared then slowly nodded. "Whatever makes you happy makes me happy, Adam."

He cleared his throat. "I know."

There was a burst of laughter from downstairs and he was grateful for the interruption. He turned back to look out the window, seeing Dominic's contented face as he chased his toddling daughter around on the lawn.

Then his gaze slid over to where Jenna and Cassandra were laughing as they watched the little girl and her father, and something lurched against his ribs. He knew Jenna would keep her word and not say anything to his sister-in-law about the money, but it hit him then how hard it must be *not* to say anything. Jenna was as protective of her family as he was of his. He admired that in her.

"I'd better get back downstairs," his mother said behind him. There was a pause. "Are you coming?"

"Give me a few more minutes. I won't be long."

He heard his mother leave but he was more tuned in to Jenna right now. She was so beautiful it made him catch his breath.

Yet it was more than that gorgeous smile and that tinkling laugh floating up to him. He'd been watching her over lunch and she seemed to fit right in with his family. She didn't gush at anyone, like one or two of his women friends had when they'd run into members of his family while out on a date. Jenna had even been a little on the shy side with them at first, but his mother and Cassandra soon had her discussing jewelry designs and it was like a flower opening, the petals peeled back to reveal the warmth of the woman inside. A warmth that held a true sincerity as she in turn asked questions of them that indicated a real interest in others. Her warmth melted something hard inside him.

Oh, hell.

Mentally, he pulled himself back at the thought and reminded himself that as much as he was coming to admire Jenna…as much as he wanted to keep on spending time with her…their being together was mostly about Chelsea, and about the money. Everything else was a bonus.

And that reminded him what his contact had said yesterday. So far there had been no hint of the money that Stewart Branson had said Liam had conned from him. It was still a mystery. And that meant no one could discount anything just yet. They had to continue trying other avenues. The money may well be tied up somewhere less obvious.

Yet as he turned to go back downstairs, he found himself wishing that he and Jenna had some sort of future together. One that was longer than his usual relationships anyway. He'd be more than happy with that.

Jenna was fully aware the moment Adam walked back out onto the terrace. He'd been quiet throughout the meal, his eyes shifting constantly to her, but not with desire or pleasure. Afterward, he'd gone inside on the pretext of getting something or other, but she had the feeling he'd needed to be alone. She hadn't followed him for that very reason.

His mother had slipped inside shortly after that, and Jenna had to wonder if Laura had gone looking for him. The other woman had only been away ten minutes or so, and on her return Laura had smiled at her, but there had been a suggestion of worry in her eyes. For Adam? And was *she* the problem? Or was she being too sensitive because Adam hadn't wanted her here today? She had to admit that if *her* family was at risk of being thrown a bombshell, she'd be on edge, too.

And yet it still hurt. Did he really think she would tackle Cassandra, his mother, or any of the other family members about Liam? She had as much to lose by doing that as he did. Besides, she'd taken a shine to Cassandra today, and would have to think hard before spoiling the other woman's happiness. Cassandra wasn't to blame for her late husband's actions.

Just then Adam came to sit beside her, and a new apprehension began to gnaw at her stomach. Surely this couldn't only be about the money? He wouldn't have left her alone with his family if that were the case. He'd have stayed by her side without fail, making sure she said nothing out of place.

So what about her being here was troubling him? It didn't take long to come to the conclusion that Adam didn't like her keeping company with his family. She was his temporary mistress, after all. And his family was the highest echelon of Australian society.

It made sense now. Hadn't he been a little remote from the moment he'd collected her before lunch? His cousin had held the door open for her, but Adam hadn't even kissed her hello when she'd slid onto the passenger seat. She'd put that down to Logan being with them. Logan Roth was another male in a family that seemed to produce men with extra good looks, charm and money, and she'd suspected his presence might have curbed Adam's actions. At least, that's what she'd told herself.

As quickly as her thoughts rushed at her, they bounced confusingly back in the other direction. She knew Adam fairly well by now. He was a man who wouldn't let anyone stop him from doing what he wanted. If he'd wanted to kiss her in front of Logan, he would have. If he had minded her being here as his mistress, he'd have refused to let her come. No, there was something not quite right going on here.

"And now I want you all to join us in a celebration," Dominic Roth said, popping open a bottle of champagne, drawing Jenna from her thoughts.

"This sounds interesting," Michael Roth teased, smiling as his eldest son began filling some glasses on a tray and passing them around.

"It's more than interesting, Dad."

"The suspense is killing me, Dominic," his mother said.

"Hang on, Mum." He finished pouring the last drink, snatched up his own glass and gently tugged a glowing Cassandra to her feet. He slipped his arm around his wife's waist. "We're going to have another baby."

It had been clear what the announcement would be, but there was still a moment's delightful surprise. Much congratulations and lots of toasts followed. Jenna felt moved that she'd been here to see all this. For all their money and connections, Adam's family was as close as her own family and with the same values. It was a comforting thought that no matter who you were, the old-fashioned ideals of love of family were still so important.

And then Jenna glanced at Adam. He seemed as glad as everyone else, yet she got the strongest feeling he was off balance about the news. Why? He loved his family more than anything. She only had to see how instinctively he'd defended Liam, and how protective he was about them not knowing about the money.

On the way back to her apartment a few hours later, he kept up an emotional distance. Logan had stayed behind, so it wasn't that his cousin was in the way this time. She felt hurt that he was putting up walls. As far as she knew, nothing had changed between them. He'd seemed happy enough yesterday before his mother's visit, but now it was like part of him wanted to keep her close, another part didn't. As if something—she didn't know what—was holding him back and it was so deep, so intense, he couldn't let himself face it.

In a way, she understood. There was something about Adam that touched an elemental piece of her, drawing emotions she didn't want to acknowledge. Her feelings were strengthening for him and she'd crossed the line, but she wasn't in love with him, thank heavens. Yet. It would be a blessing when this was finally over. Perhaps now was even the time to suggest that very thing….

Back at her place, she started edging to what was on her mind. "I'm sorry, Adam. It might have helped the situation with Chelsea, but I shouldn't have gone with you today. You didn't want me there. I know it and so do you."

There was an interminable pause. "It's not that. It's…" The line of his jaw flexed.

"Yes?"

"I've got some stuff on my mind, that's all."

"Maybe I can help?"

He stood there a moment longer, then, "Come here," he muttered, pulling her into his arms to hold her tight.

"Adam, I—"

He silenced her with a kiss.

And she let him.

They made love, but during it all he still kept up some sort of barrier between them. She tried to reach him on an emotional level, but he was in a place she couldn't follow. He was satisfying her, no doubt about that, yet it was like he was being driven to take her, not driven to make them one, like the previous times they'd made love.

Afterward he went into the bathroom and she tried not to think at all. She needed to regain her sense of balance, but she couldn't do that when thoughts of Adam and this demon that suddenly seemed to be riding him were on her mind.

When he came back out of the bathroom, his face was as white as the towel he'd wrapped around his hips.

She sat up. "What's the matter?"

"The condom was broken."

"What! How?"

"I'm not going into bloody detail. It broke."

"Oh, my God," she whispered.

He just stood there.

Then it started to hit her. She was terrified and yet…she felt the tiniest of thrills. "I could be pregnant already."

"Don't say that," he grated harshly, throwing off the towel and reaching for his pants, bringing her back to reality. His movements were jerky. He was clearly upset.

Jenna got off the bed and went to him. "Look, don't worry about it," she said, trying to stay calm herself. "It'll be fine." She put her hand on his arm.

He tossed it off like he'd tossed away the towel a minute ago. "You know that, do you?"

She was taken aback. "No, I don't know that," she said firmly, aware one of them had to keep their cool. "But I do know that panicking about it won't help the situation."

He gave a hesitant pause that was so uncharacteristic of him. "You're right, of course," he muttered, then continued to finish dressing.

Clearly he was going home and she had no problem with that. But was he going because he had something to do? Or because he wanted to get away from her? The latter filled her with dismay. Did he think so little of her that he'd hate her to have his baby? The reminder that she was only a warm body in his bed brought a hard lump to her throat.

She'd been a fool to think it had been anything other than sex. God, she shouldn't be surprised.

"I'll call you," he said, giving her a brief, hard kiss with a slight lashing of gentleness, as if he just couldn't quite let go of her...yet.

After he left, she sat there and wondered if he really would call her this time. And would it be because he wanted to? Or because she could stir up trouble for his family?

Driving home, Adam felt sick at the thought of the broken condom. Dammit, he should have taken more care, only he hadn't really been concentrating on that. He'd just wanted Jenna and had been trying not to think about anything else. He'd wanted to bury himself in her body and forget that it was coming up to the fifth anniversary of losing his wife and child. He wanted to forget that Dominic and Cassandra were now having another child and that he really was very, very happy for them, but that it only served to remind him he'd lost so much himself.

And now look what his lapse had done!

Jenna could be pregnant.

She could be carrying *his* child.

He couldn't go through that again. A loss like he'd had wasn't something a person could overcome. He could still see Maddie's ecstatic face telling him she was pregnant and the lump of emotion the thought of her carrying his child had brought. She'd been such a lovely person. She'd only wanted to be a good wife and a good mother. And she would have excelled at both.

If she'd been given the chance.

At the next intersection, he turned his car around and headed toward the cemetery.

Nine

Jenna went to work the next day but there were no calls from Adam. Her heart sank that evening when he didn't drop by her apartment, either. He finally phoned her at home, but their conversation was stilted. He was distancing himself from her. Everything had been heading toward this, but clearly the broken condom had been the final straw for him. Whether he'd want to continue the facade for Todd and Chelsea's sake, she wasn't sure.

And if she was pregnant?

She fought not to stress about it. Maybe it was burying her head in the sand, but right now she had too much else to worry about. Nor would she let herself think about what Adam's reaction would be if he were to become a father, though if it was anything like his reaction now she didn't think he was going to like it. Nonetheless, she took comfort that Adam was the kind of man who took his responsibilities seriously. She would worry about it *if* it happened. Not before.

Keeping busy after that was a necessity, especially when he didn't call her at work the next day, or the next evening, nor were there any messages left on her cell phone. But on Wednesday evening her doorbell rang and her heart jumped in her throat. Adam was here! She raced to answer it.

She could feel her face fall with disappointment when she saw her sister-in-law at the door.

Vicki wrinkled her nose. "You look like you were expecting someone else. Sorry, I should have called first."

Jenna summoned a smile. "You're welcome here anytime, Vicki. Come on in."

"I won't stay long if you've got someone else coming soon," she said, stepping into the apartment.

Jenna realized it was fortuitous that Adam wasn't here. It was best to keep them all apart, not because she thought Adam might say something about the money, but because she didn't want Vicki seeing how her relationship with him was falling apart. Right now it was just so personal.

She shook her head and tried to appear unconcerned. "No, I'm not expecting anyone else." She gestured for Vicki to take a seat on the couch. "So, what have you done with the children?"

"I dropped them off at Mum and Dad's place." Vicki's parents had died when she was a teenager, so she considered the older Bransons her parents now. "I told them I wanted to go to the library and get some books and that it was best if I didn't take the kids."

Jenna had an uneasy feeling. "This all sounds rather mysterious."

"It is."

"Would you like a cup of coffee first?" She was starting

to get heart palpitations that Adam might arrive now, but she couldn't be impolite.

"No, thanks." Vicki took a letter out of her handbag. "You might be able to help me figure this out, Jenna. The quarterly bank statement came today for our mortgage and I'm confused. It says that we're behind on payments. Worse, that we still owe three hundred and fifty thousand dollars." Her forehead creased. "Last year we only had fifty thousand dollars left on the loan, so I don't know why this extra amount has been added. And such a large amount, too."

Jenna lowered her lashes, trying to appear as if she knew nothing. "Let me see the statement." Vicki handed it over, but Jenna already knew what she'd find. "Yes, that's what it says."

If only Stewart had thought to have mail from the bank sent directly to him. Of course, he'd been a mess when he'd left the country and no doubt it hadn't occurred to him. Anyway, Vicki had said "quarterly" bank statements. Just their luck the end of the quarter had been now.

"It has to be a mistake, right?" Vicki said.

Jenna tried to appear unconcerned. "I'm sure it is."

Vicki looked relieved. "That's what I thought. I didn't get to open the letter until tonight. Otherwise I would have phoned them to check."

Thank God she hadn't. "Did you mention this to Stewart?"

"He's only contactable via email at the moment, but no, I didn't want to worry him when he's so far away. And I didn't want to worry Mum and Dad, so I didn't tell them, either."

Jenna nodded, greatly relieved on both counts. "Good thinking. No need to worry any of them."

Vicki's brows drew together. "The trouble is it's my turn

to help out with the lunches at the school tomorrow and I'll be busy all day with that. I won't be able to phone the bank in private." She paused. "Do you think you could phone them for me tomorrow sometime?"

Jenna knew instantly that the bank wouldn't speak to her about it, but she needed time to think about this latest development. "Sure, leave it with me. I'll see what I can find out and give you a call tomorrow night." If she could just stretch things out, give Adam time to end the investigation and put the money back, then perhaps Vicki need know nothing of what had transpired.

"Come for dinner after work," Vicki said. "It would be lovely for the girls to see you again. They've missed you."

Jenna's heart softened. "I've missed them, too."

Vicki left after that and Jenna sat on the couch and worried herself crazy. She had Stewart's email address, so she should probably contact him about it all, but that would only upset him, being so far away from home and unable to explain it all to Vicki in person.

Damn her brother for letting himself get involved with Liam Roth. And damn her brother for getting *her* involved in this, as well. It was affecting too many lives now. Perhaps destroying them.

An hour later Jenna couldn't stand it any longer. She'd been debating whether to go see Adam tomorrow morning at his office about what Vicki had told her, or to go see him now. She chose the latter, unable to sleep not knowing what was going on with him, both personally and with the money.

She didn't phone him first though, frightened he might put her off coming. It was only on the way over in her car it occurred to her that another woman might be there with him. Her heart constricted at the thought. Well, then, at least she'd know it was officially over.

The concierge was pleasant, but he insisted on phoning the penthouse first, and she was fine with that. In the quietness of the foyer, she could hear Adam's voice as he answered. There was the slightest pause when he heard who wanted to see him, though Jenna was at least grateful the concierge didn't seem to notice. Or he was probably too well trained to show it.

"Go on up, Ms. Branson."

Adam was waiting when she stepped out of the elevator. Her step faltered as she walked toward him. He looked as gorgeous as ever, but his face was slightly pale and that caught at her heartstrings. Was the thought of her being pregnant making him look like this?

She frowned. "Adam, are you okay?"

He avoided her eyes as he leaned down and kissed her, not on her mouth but on the *cheek*. "I'm fine." He gestured for her to take a seat on the couch, but she preferred to stand.

She surreptitiously glanced around, noting the papers spread on the dining table where he'd obviously been working. She was intensely relieved not to see any signs of another woman's presence. "I'm interrupting your work."

He grimaced. "The last couple of days have been… hectic."

"I see," she said slowly. Then she took a deep breath. "Adam, my sister-in-law came to see me tonight." She explained about the bank statement. "So I was wondering if you knew anything more about the money?"

His face shuttered. "No, I'm afraid not. It's still being investigated."

"Oh." She frowned. "It's taking a long time, isn't it?"

He shot her a glare. "That's the way it is sometimes."

"I see." She drew herself up straighter. Clearly she wasn't going to get anything more out of him about this right now. "Please let me know if you find out anything."

"I will."

He was like a stranger, and she couldn't stand it any longer. Her niggling doubts suddenly took over. "Look, Adam, if we're finished please tell me now."

"What the hell!" His brow knitted together. "What gave you that idea?"

She faced him fully. "Oh, just a little matter of you not wanting to be with me, that's all."

And the kiss on the cheek before.

And the condom breaking.

His gaze held hers. "I *do* want to be with you."

She didn't let herself acknowledge relief. "Really? You're very good at putting up walls."

A curious look passed over his face. "What are you on about?"

"You've stayed away all this week, yet last week you couldn't get enough of me."

"I still want you," he growled. "Don't doubt that."

"Then why aren't you showing it?" she challenged, relieved but not.

He heaved a sigh. "Look, with Dominic back in the office we've had a lot of work to catch up on. We're working on something new, too. It's eating into my evenings."

She searched his eyes, wanting him to tell her the truth even if it wasn't what she wanted to hear. He seemed sincere, yet… "Do you realize you've never stayed overnight at my apartment?"

He stiffened. "So?"

"It's your way of keeping your distance, isn't it?"

His brows drew into a straight line. "I've let you stay here overnight. How can that be keeping you at a distance?"

"Don't try and confuse the issue. This is about *you* staying with *me,* not *me* staying with *you.*"

He gave a short laugh. "There's a difference?"

"You know there is." She would stand here until he acknowledged it. "See, you're doing it even now. You're trying to twist things around so I won't notice that you're holding yourself back from me."

Another short laugh. "Obviously, it's not working."

"Don't make fun."

He sent her a sharp look, then ran his fingers through his hair. "What do you want from me, Jenna?"

"Honesty, Adam. Just plain old honesty."

Several seconds crept by.

"So you want honesty?"

She braced herself. "Yes."

He expelled a breath. "Yesterday was the fifth anniversary of my wife's death," he said, making her gasp. "*That's* why I've stayed away this week."

Her breath deserted her for a couple of seconds. "Oh, Adam, I'm sorry. I didn't know."

"I didn't expect you to know," he said in a low voice.

She felt a twinge that he had shut her out, but then, he didn't owe it to her to tell her this. It was such a private thing. She just wished… "I've made it worse for you."

He took steps toward her and pulled her close. "You didn't," he muttered into her hair. "I've been trying to keep busy and work through it all."

Her heart ached for his ache.

"Tell me about your wife." She felt him startle against her and she frowned as she eased back. "You don't want to talk about her?"

"No, it's not that. It's just…no other woman has asked me to talk about Maddie before."

Her heart swelled. "I'm glad I'm the first."

Squeezing her hands, he stepped back and went to stand a few feet away near the dining table, putting distance between them, but this time she understood his need to stand alone.

He lifted his shoulders. "Where to begin?"

"What sort of person was she?" Jenna asked, helping him out, curious all the same.

"Beautiful." He smiled at himself, then inclined his head. "A beautiful person. She loved life and it showed. She used to giggle a lot. A schoolgirl type of giggle. She was such a practical joker."

"She sounds like she was great fun."

"She was. The day she was…" his eyes filled with pain "…killed, she had all these balloons in the car. I assume she was bringing them home to plant around the house as a surprise. The police don't know why she swerved into a light pole, but we think it might have been because of the balloons. A witness said she saw Maddie trying to push one over the backseat just before the accident." He took a shuddering breath, looking bleak. "God, it seems like only yesterday she was here with me. Yet at the same time it seems like forever."

A lump welled in her throat. "Oh, Adam."

He gave a hard laugh. "Did you really want to hear all this?"

She went to him then, slipped her arms around him and hugged him tight, wanting to take away his pain. "Yes," she whispered, leaning up and kissing him tenderly on the mouth. "Adam, I'm so sorry for your loss."

"I know."

"Would it be wrong of me to make love to you right now?"

His eyes darkened. "I think it would be very right."

She kissed him again, then took his hand and led him

into his bedroom where she stripped the clothes from both their bodies and made love to him, needing to help him forget his pain.

They both fell asleep, but in the early hours of the morning she woke and lay there curled up beside him, thinking about what he'd told her. Until now she hadn't really had time to reflect on Adam being a widower. She'd had so many other things of concern that thinking beyond any immediate problems hadn't really been an option.

Now she at least knew what was going on with him. Their relationship wouldn't lead anywhere in the long run, but she was pleased she at least understood some of his actions. He'd lost the love of his life and he wasn't about to settle for second best. Sadly, to him all women were considered second best…and that included *her*.

At the thought, she knew she needed some breathing space. Careful not to wake him, she slid out of bed and dressed quietly, then crept out of the apartment, leaving him sleeping heavily.

It was only as she drove home that something occurred to her. Adam had said nothing about the possibility of her being pregnant, and she hadn't brought it up, either. It was as if he'd shut it out of his mind. Thinking back on the terrible week that he'd had, there was no way she'd remind him now.

By midmorning Jenna was over her need for time-out and was eager to see Adam again, so she was delighted when he called her at work on her cell phone.

"How about lunch today?" he asked. "Can you get away around noon?"

"That would be wonderful."

He sounded pleased to be seeing her again, and she felt the same. She'd decided to take this moment by moment, but it made her feel good to know he was putting in an effort to be with her.

Except that when Jenna entered the restaurant, she was dismayed to see Adam wasn't alone. He was sitting at a table with Todd and Chelsea.

He pushed to his feet as soon as he saw her and weaved through the tables, his eyes set on her face. "Sorry," he muttered, kissing her briefly on the mouth. "They were already here and I couldn't ignore them. Now smile."

She pasted on a smile as he guided her to the table, but Jenna was wondering if Chelsea had known Adam would be here today. It might only have taken a well-placed phone call to his personal assistant to find out.

The other pair welcomed her in a friendly manner, but she couldn't help notice the friendliness didn't reach Chelsea's eyes. Then the other woman's gaze flickered down over Jenna's pants and top that until this moment had felt more than passable. Now she felt like something the dog had dragged in.

No one had ordered yet, and while they made their decision Chelsea seemed to go into overdrive again. She laughed loudly at something on the menu, pointing it out to Adam in a flirtatious way, then asked the waiter for another glass of wine as she tossed back the remains of her half-empty glass in a way that actually made Todd's mouth tighten. At that point Jenna suspected the other pair's presence hadn't been by design. They really had been about to lunch together, and now Chelsea was thrown by the appearance of her and Adam.

And then from over at another table in the corner, a baby suddenly started to cry and Chelsea seemed to freeze a moment before her eyes flew to her husband's face. Something passed between them.

"Chels, don't—" Todd began.

Chelsea pushed to her feet. "Shut up, Todd," she choked in a low, pain-filled voice. "Just shut up!" Grabbing her purse, she rushed out of the restaurant.

There was a stunned silence at their table.

Todd surged to his feet, but paused to look at them both. "I have to go," he muttered, then twisted around and hurried after his wife.

Adam and Jenna sat in a pocket of silence for a few seconds, their gazes following Todd. The noise in the restaurant remained static, so it didn't appear that others had noticed anything out of the ordinary.

"What the hell was that about?" Adam finally said.

"I'm not sure."

Outside the restaurant, they saw Chelsea flag down a taxi and almost fall onto the backseat. Todd reached it just as the vehicle drove away. Like a defeated man, he stood and watched as his wife slipped out of sight, then he slowly turned and came back into the restaurant.

He was pale as he flopped down onto his chair. "I'm sorry you saw that."

Adam frowned at his friend. "What's up, Todd?"

Todd winced. "I didn't want to say anything before but…" He lowered his gaze and took a deep breath before looking up again. "About two months ago we found out Chelsea was pregnant," he said, making Jenna gasp. She felt Adam stiffen beside her. "We were both thrilled. Then…she lost the baby and…" His eyes held anguish as he focused on Adam, sharing his pain with his friend. "Things haven't been the same since. That baby crying just now tipped her over the edge."

Jenna tried not to think how *she* would feel in the same circumstances. Not when she might be pregnant herself. Oh, God, she wasn't going there.

Surprisingly, Adam didn't speak. Could he be thinking

about *her* carrying his child? Or was he silenced by his friend's heartache?

She dared not look at him as she stepped in the breach and said sympathetically, "I'm so sorry, Todd."

The other man inclined his head. "Thanks." Then he looked back at Adam. "I didn't want to say anything to you, Adam." He paused. "You can see why, can't you?"

Adam seemed to pull himself together. "Yes, of course," he said somewhat abruptly, but he looked pale, and Jenna was reminded how seriously to heart Adam took this friendship with Todd. They were very close.

"Chels hasn't been the same since it happened," Todd was saying now. "She seems to have gone off track somehow. We've both been putting on a brave face, but I know it's eating her up inside."

A couple of seconds ticked by and no one spoke, but both men looked extremely worried. Jenna had to admit Chelsea didn't seem like a stalker now, just sad. The other woman had a wonderful husband who loved her and hopefully many more babies in their future, but first they had to get through this.

"Have you tried talking to her?" she asked, wanting to help.

Todd gave a short shake of his head. "No. Every time I do she starts to cry and I feel helpless, so I end up letting her be."

Jenna's brows drew together. "She needs you, Todd. You really should go after her."

"She'll only start crying again."

"Then let her cry." She tilted her head at him. "And perhaps you ought to have a good cry right along with her. It might be the only way to deal with this."

Todd blinked.

Adam cleared his throat. "Jenna's right. You both need to work through your grief before you can move on."

There was a pause. "I guess we do have to start somewhere." A determined light grew in Todd's eyes as he rose to his feet. "Thanks, you two." The sincerity in his eyes encompassed them both before he left the restaurant.

Jenna silently wished the pair well.

Then her gaze returned to the man beside her. "Looks like we've got our answer why Chelsea has been acting so strange."

Adam was trying to cope with the shaft of pain in his chest. Todd and Chelsea had lost a baby? Todd had gone through the same thing *he* had gone through? He could understand why his friend hadn't wanted to tell him. Todd would be remembering Adam's darkest days.

Of course, Todd would also be aware of one big difference. He at least still had a wife to help him get through this.

Unlike Adam.

Thank heavens he'd thought to cut Todd off before he'd said anything more in front of Jenna. No one knew about Maddie having been pregnant when she'd died. No one except him and Todd and the hospital staff. Todd had promised he'd never tell a soul, not even Chelsea. Adam fully believed that he'd kept his word. Chelsea wouldn't be acting so foolish toward her husband's best friend if she'd known they had losing a baby in common.

A baby.

Jenna could be pregnant.

"I suspected there was something more going on between them."

Jenna's words jolted him back into the moment. He scowled at her. "You didn't say anything to me about that."

She lifted one slim shoulder. "It was a hunch, nothing more. It wouldn't have helped the situation. We couldn't do anything about it."

He thought about that, and admitted, "Yeah, I got the same hunch when Todd invited us to their vacation home. He told me Chelsea had some sort of female problems. He didn't say it was something serious."

Jenna began to chew her lip. "I think she might have phoned me once. It was the evening we came back from their vacation home."

"What!"

"When I answered, no one spoke. It was quiet for a few seconds, then they hung up. I still think it was Chelsea. I suspect she was trying to see if you were with me."

"Why the hell didn't you tell me?"

"It was nothing. Not really. And I had no proof." She sighed. "Poor Chelsea."

He took a calming breath. "Yes." Chelsea's grief had made her look foolish, that was all.

"I guess you were just a distraction from her losing the baby." There was compassion in Jenna's voice. She considered him. "I don't think she'll be after you anymore, do you?"

She was right. "No, I don't think so, either." And that was a great relief. "But she probably still needs to see us together for a while longer. At least until she gets her head in a good place."

"Good idea."

He suddenly felt the need to say more. "Anyway, I don't plan on giving you up just yet, Jenna." And she'd better not think otherwise. To make sure, he reminded her, "This isn't only about Chelsea. We need to get the money sorted out with your brother." There was no escaping that fact. "That's the reason we came together in the first place."

Her gaze faltered. "True." She moistened her mouth. "So, this means I owe you two more weeks of my time. While you find the money for Stewart, that is."

His jaw clenched and he wanted to say that as far as he was concerned, finding the money wasn't for Stewart. It was to clear his own brother's name, if he could.

And one of them was going to lose big-time.

Just then, he caught sight of the waiter coming their way. "Let's have some lunch."

She hesitated. "Actually, Adam, I'm not very hungry right now. I hope you don't mind."

He realized he'd lost his appetite, too. "I'm not hungry, either." He pushed to his feet and helped her out of her chair. "Come on. I'll walk you back to work."

As they left the restaurant he noticed his cell phone had a couple of messages from the private investigator. He didn't mention it to Jenna, but his heart had just slammed right into his ribs.

At Vicki's place that evening, once they'd had dinner and the children had gone to bed, Jenna relayed the information she'd learned from the bank. To make herself feel better about deceiving her sister-in-law, she'd phoned the bank this afternoon, and as suspected had been told they would only deal with their customer. Jenna had mentioned that Vicki would call tomorrow then, and was told that the account was in Stewart's name and only Stewart could discuss the account with them.

"Really?" Vicki said with dismay. "They won't talk to me about it? It's *my* house, for goodness' sake!"

"Yes, but the account is in Stewart's name only."

Vicki frowned. "We never realized it would be a problem."

Jenna wondered if Stewart had done that deliberately.

Of course, he really couldn't have known he would lose his money. No person in their right mind would put their house up as collateral if they thought they were going to lose it.

Vicki nodded, still clearly worried, but trying not to show it. "Thanks for checking for me, sweetie. I appreciate it."

"That's okay. I'm glad to help."

"I'll email Stewart tonight and tell him there's a problem with the account," Vicki said. "He can email the bank himself and give them permission to talk to me while he's out of the country. Once he's back we'll have to see about putting the house in both names."

"Sounds good," Jenna said, though she suspected Stewart's first action would be to call or email *her* about it. He didn't know she had forced Adam to help sort this out, and he would be frantic when he received Vicki's email in case his wife discovered the truth about the money.

No doubt he would come up with a plan for delaying the inevitable. Knowing her brother, he'd soon realize he only had to pretend to Vicki about putting her name down as a contact. Once he returned to Australia, he'd be hoping to replace most of the money himself, though he had no idea the money might still be repaid out of Liam's account—and she wouldn't tell him. She didn't want him to get his hopes up on something that may not come to be.

And why the heck was she being so considerate of Stewart at the moment? She didn't feel too kindly toward him right now. Either way he'd have covered his own butt.

"So you're telling me you can't find any trace of the money?" Adam ground out. Today had been one shock after another. First Todd and Chelsea at lunch, now the forensic accountant was meeting him here in his penthouse before dinner rather than risk him coming to the office. He wanted his family knowing nothing about this.

"That's right, Mr. Roth. And believe me, I've had my people check thoroughly. They know all the tricks and all the places money can be hidden in secret accounts, and there's nothing to be found. Absolutely nothing."

It was as he'd suspected. "So Stewart Branson didn't give any money to my brother?"

"No."

"So it's a con job," he said, his lips flattening with anger. And Jenna was in on it, along with her brother. He should have listened to his gut instinct from the beginning.

"It certainly looks like it. I have some pretty damning evidence."

Adam scowled. "Evidence? But I thought you just said you couldn't find anything?"

"I didn't. But I *have* discovered something very interesting. Did you know that Stewart Branson…"

By the time Adam finished listening, he was more than angry. He was ice-cold furious. He latched on to the feeling, taking pleasure in the pain, knowing it was far better than thinking about any other matter with Jenna that might be totally out of his control. *Nothing* was going to be out of his control again where she was concerned. Not ever again.

Ten

Jenna left Vicki's house fairly early with the excuse that she had to work tomorrow. There had been no calls on her cell phone, and she wanted to get home now to see if there were any messages from Adam on her answering machine. After what had happened at the restaurant today, she thought he might have contacted her to talk more about Todd and Chelsea.

Adam was waiting at her apartment door when she stepped out from the elevator. Joy swept through her.

She smiled as she came toward him. "Have you been waiting long?"

"Long enough," was the curt reply.

She looked at his set face, and her smile slipped. Perhaps she'd heard wrong? It could have merely been the acoustics here in the hallway. Or maybe something else had cropped up with his friends?

She smiled again. A smaller one this time. "I didn't know you were coming. I've been out to dinner."

His mouth tightened, but up closer she could see something flicker in eyes that had a definite hardness to them. "Just open the door," he said in a clipped tone.

She did.

Something was seriously wrong. Was he angry because she hadn't been home waiting for his arrival? That made her even angrier with herself now for hurrying home. She wasn't going to pander to him, she decided, going over and putting her handbag on the couch.

"So, what's up?" She angled her chin as she turned to face him. She might be his mistress, but she wasn't about to take the brunt of his bad mood.

"You are," he snapped. "You're a real piece of work, lady."

Air rushed into her lungs. "Wh-what do you mean?"

His top lip curled. "So innocent. You play the part well."

She stiffened. "What are you talking about?"

"Remember how I met with that business acquaintance last Saturday?"

"Yes."

"It was about the money."

A light dimmed inside her. He'd said his appointment was business, and she supposed it was…but to not mention it had been about the money was deceiving.

She drew herself up. "Tell me."

"That guy had been through everything and checked everywhere to see if your brother had given Liam any money. Up until last Saturday there was still no trace of any transaction, but we decided to keep on trying. By this afternoon he'd exhausted all avenues and concluded no such transaction had ever taken place."

Her brain stumbled. "That can't be," she whispered.

"Can't it?"

She thought for a moment, then something occurred to her. "Just because you found nothing doesn't prove a thing."

"No, but I found out something very interesting in the meantime. Your brother has a gambling problem."

She could only blink. Her mouth tried to work but wouldn't.

His lips twisted. "You're surprised? Or surprised that I know?"

"Wh-what?"

"You and your brother have been caught out, Jenna. Admit it. Your brother lost the money gambling, and you both concocted this scheme to get me to give you money so that he can put it back in his bank account for the mortgage. It was brilliant. A dead man can't talk, can he? Liam can't deny the charges and I can't prove conclusively that the money *didn't* change hands. Not yet anyway."

She was trying to get her head around this. He was saying that Stewart had gambled the money away and hadn't given any money to Liam to invest at all? That he had made up all this to get the grief-stricken Roth family to replace the money? And worst of all that *she'd* planned this with her brother?

"You're not serious," was all she could manage.

"Dead serious, my sweet."

And he was.

She shook her head. "Apart from knowing I've done nothing wrong, I don't believe what you're saying about Stewart. You're just trying to get out of paying. You're making it all up."

He ripped some papers from his jacket pocket and thrust

them at her. "I have it all in writing. Read it and see. You can't dispute it."

Her hands shook as she took the paperwork and began to read. She could feel the blood drain from every cell in her body. It was all there in black and white.

"Your brother has been gambling under an assumed name so that no one would trace it back to him. He's been living another life. Stewart Branson is as clean as a whistle and that's why it took so long to discover this."

She shook her head. "I don't believe it," she muttered, more to try and convince herself that the paperwork in front of her was a bunch of lies. How could it *not* be?

"I'm sure," he said sarcastically. "Hell, you probably increased the amount and asked for more money than he needed, intending to put the money back in his account *and* pay off this fancy new apartment you've bought yourself."

That last bit brought her up short. "I took out a mortgage on this apartment." She was proud of buying this place from her earnings. It was all aboveboard and honestly earned.

"Which you could still have paid off early and no one would be the wiser." A second ticked by. "You've been caught out, Jenna. Admit it."

How could she admit to something she hadn't done?

"What if I told you I didn't know anything about Stewart's gambling? What if I believed he was telling me the truth?"

"I'd say you were lying."

"You *want* to believe that, Adam."

"No, I *have* to believe it. This scam is serious business. Three hundred thousand dollars is a lot of money."

"I don't want any money that doesn't belong to Stewart, Adam."

"You've suddenly found some principles, have you?"

"Obviously you'll think what you want." She steadied her breathing, then considered him. "You believe I lied to you, but you lied to me too, Adam."

That brought him up short. "When?"

"When I asked you last night you said you didn't know anything further about the money. You didn't mention what the appointment last Saturday was about, nor that there were further questions about not being able to trace anything."

Nothing on his face relented. "Rule Number One. Don't tell your enemy your game plan."

Hurt sliced through her. "So I'm your enemy now, am I?"

"Were you ever anything else?"

She gave a soft gasp. "Thanks very much."

For a split second he looked pained, then he glared at her. "You used me, Jenna. You used me to try and get money out of me to help your brother, and probably some for yourself, as well. So don't try and make it sound like *I'm* the one who did anything wrong."

This man in front of her was a stranger, his face hard, his eyes like steel. He wasn't about to relent. He was totally convinced of Stewart's guilt.

Of *her* guilt.

"Are you going to the police about this?" she asked, not in fear for herself, but for Stewart. If he really did have a gambling problem…if she'd inadvertently made demands of Adam Roth on his behalf…where would it lead?

A light of triumph entered his eyes. He thought she was guilty and running scared. He gave a sharp shake of his head. "No, I want to spare my family any further pain."

Her shoulders sagged with relief.

"But if I'm pushed, then I *will* go to the police," he warned. "Don't doubt that. So I suggest your brother gets some help. He's been dealing with some unsavory types and next time he may not be able to pay them off. If he lands in debt with them again, they'll no doubt sort him out."

"Oh, my God." Her voice quavered from deep inside. This was getting worse every minute. It sounded as if Stewart's life could be in danger in future.

There was a pause, and Adam almost looked sorry for her. "He needs help with his addiction, Jenna."

"I know," she murmured, finally admitting out loud that it must be true about Stewart.

"And you need help, too. You can't go around conning money from people."

She thrust out her chin. "I only wanted repaid what I thought belonged to Stewart."

"So you say," he mocked. "By the way, I said I'd merely look into the money. I didn't say I'd pay it back. Ever." A vein pulsed near his temple. "I owe you nothing."

"And I don't know you at all, do I?"

"No, you don't." He twisted away and slammed out the door.

Jenna sank onto the couch, a sense of pain so intense, so acute she could feel it like a very real punch in her heart. And there was only one reason for it. For the first time she knew.

She loved Adam Roth.

Bile sat in Adam's throat as he drove home. He should have known Jenna was too good to be true. All that pretending to be concerned about her brother losing his home. And her concern for her sister-in-law and nieces. It had all been lies. Sure, she'd been concerned, but only because she was in on it with her brother. Her sister-in-law might even be a part of it, too. How many others had the Bransons tried to scam?

God, what a fool he'd been. He'd actually thought she was like his mother and Cassandra. He'd actually thought Jenna had integrity, even if it had been misplaced with her brother.

He'd been wrong.

Totally.

It would never happen again, he decided, hardening what was left of his pride. No woman was ever going to get the slightest chance to make a fool of him again. He was a playboy through and through, and that's the way it was going to stay.

And whenever he thought of Jenna Branson in the future, he'd imagine a mere notch on his bedpost…even if it killed him.

Jenna wasn't sure how long she sat there after Adam had gone. Time didn't matter. Not when her heart was breaking. How could Adam think this of her? How could he believe she would have anything to do with deceiving anyone, let alone him? It hurt to think about it.

And then there was Stewart.

No wonder her brother had told her to let things be when she'd first suggested approaching the Roths. He'd known he hadn't given Liam Roth any money. How fortuitous for him that Liam's funeral had been on the television the day he'd come to her apartment. It had given him the excuse he'd needed to justify both his wan appearance and his newly increased mortgage. He'd put on a thoroughly convincing act.

The only good thing now was that Stewart must have used the mortgage money to repay his gambling debts. Otherwise they'd be after him…perhaps even Vicki and the children. The thought made her feel sick.

God, Adam had been right that it would happen again

if Stewart didn't get help. Gambling was an addiction. She hadn't had personal experience of it until now, and she wasn't exactly sure what it all meant, but she suspected he wouldn't be able to control it without some sort of outside assistance and support. Knowing Stewart, he probably wasn't about to do that unless pushed.

Her mouth firmed with determination as she jumped to her feet and went to turn on her computer. Her brother was going to get one hell of an email from her right now. She wasn't going to mention her affair, but she would tell him everything else that had occurred since the day she'd met Adam at the races. It seemed another lifetime ago now instead of mere weeks.

And then she wanted answers.

She did that, then changed into more comfortable clothes before making herself a cup of coffee. She waited. An hour later her telephone rang.

It was Stewart.

"Jenna, what the hell have you done?" he demanded down the line, sounding as if he was in the room with her and not in the Middle East.

She wished he was. She'd box his ears, as well as give him an earful. "Me? Good God, Stewart! You're the one who lied and cheated. Why on earth did you concoct such a story?"

She heard him curse. "It would have been okay if you hadn't confronted Adam Roth. I had it all worked out. I've made some money, and I was about to bank a lump sum, but now you've got us implicated in some sort of elaborate swindle."

She couldn't believe he was blaming *her*. "Maybe you should have been honest with me in the first place," she said through gritted teeth.

"And what about Vicki?" he said, ignoring her comment.

"Did you tell her anything about this? Is that how come she got her hands on the bank statement?" he demanded, his words telling her Vicki must have already emailed him tonight about him making it a joint account.

This so wasn't fair. *She* was getting blamed from all angles. "The bank sent the quarterly statement to the house because *you* forgot all about it."

There was a pause. "I can't be expected to think of everything, you know."

"Well, you should have preempted that and had the statement sent to the Middle East, or even to me. It's fortunate for you that the account isn't in joint names, or Vicki would be frantic by now. And no, she doesn't know about any of this. I've only just found out myself." And she wasn't over the shock of it.

"You're not going to tell her, are you?"

"No. *You* are."

"Don't be ridiculous, Jenna. It's sorted out now. You said in your email that Roth wasn't going to press charges. I'll be making enough money over the next few months to put it all back on the mortgage. Vicki doesn't need to hear about this. Let it rest."

It was tempting to let things ride, but she knew she couldn't do that to her brother. She loved him too much.

"You're fooling yourself, Stewart. You've got a gambling addiction and it isn't going away. Eventually you'll get the urge to gamble again and who knows what will happen next time? Some of those people might decide to play dirty if you don't pay up."

He gave a hard laugh. "You've been watching too many gangster movies."

"Have I?"

There was dead silence.

"It'll be fine, Jenna," he said tightly. "Trust me."

"I'm sorry. I can't. Next time you might lose the house. And you might lose Vicki and the girls. They deserve better."

The words hung in the air.

He made a sound like a groan. "I can't tell her, Jenna."

"You don't have a choice," she pointed out, then heard herself say, "If you don't tell her, then *I* will."

"You wouldn't!"

"Yes, I would." But surely he wouldn't let her. When it all came down to it, if Vicki had to know, then he had to be the one to tell his wife.

"Okay, you win, sis. *You* do it."

"Wh-what!" Jenna almost dropped the phone.

"Look, I'm thousands of miles away, and telling Vicki this in a phone call isn't the way to go. You're absolutely right that she deserves better. She deserves to hear this directly. If you do this, you can answer any questions she has and judge how she is taking it. I don't want her to do anything silly."

She blanched. He'd well and truly called her bluff... and yet she wasn't beyond a bit of manipulation herself. "Okay, I'll do it. But only if you promise to get help for your addiction as soon as you get home." She took a moment to let that sink in. "And I'm going to tell Mum and Dad, as well."

"You can't do that!"

"They deserve to know, Stewart," she said, making sure her tone held no nonsense. She wouldn't relent on this. "I tell them as well, or I don't say anything and I let *you* sort it out when you get back, and by then you'll probably have Vicki frantic with worry. She might even hop on a plane and come and see you."

He swore. "Okay. Do it." He paused, then muttered, "I never knew you were such a hard person, sis."

Not hard enough apparently, she decided as they finished the call and hung up. A thank-you would have been nice.

The next day Jenna took the day off work, asked Vicki to leave the kids with a babysitter, then she met them all at her parents' place where she told them everything about Stewart and Liam Roth. She left out any mention of her and Adam's relationship, and she definitely didn't tell them she was in love with him. She'd leave it for a while, then let them think things had cooled and died a natural death. At least she was no longer a mistress.

Of course, telling her family about Stewart was one of the hardest things she'd ever had to do. The enormity and complexity of Stewart's gambling problem upset everyone. After the shock had worn off, it was clear they were all going to support him. Her parents had fifty thousand dollars they offered to put into their son's mortgage account, but that was their retirement money and Vicki flatly refused, stating that Stewart had to take responsibility for all this. Jenna had always loved Vicki, but at that moment she admired the other woman for everything she stood for.

Mother and wife.

Later, Jenna decided to leave them to talk. She'd had enough of it all and just wanted to go home and lie down and *not think*. She'd spent such a restless night going over what she had to say. It was upsetting.

As she walked to the front door, Jenna discovered her mother saw more than she'd realized.

"Adam Roth," Joyce began. "He seems a good man."

She tried not to react. "He is, Mum. Very good."

Her mother searched her face. "He doesn't hold your brother's gambling problem against you, does he?"

She winced inwardly. "No, of course not," she lied,

then kissed her cheek. "I have to go. I've got to finish up something at work." She moved to leave.

"Jenna?"

Her steps stopped. "Yes?"

"You're a good sister. Thank you for helping Stewart."

Love rose inside Jenna's chest. She hugged her mother one last time. "Thanks, Mum," she murmured, warmth staying with her until she arrived home at her apartment.

Then it suddenly all felt so empty.

Just like her.

Eleven

Over the next few weeks Adam threw himself into his job. He'd stayed in Melbourne to help his father run the business while Dominic had been away on his second honeymoon, but now he went back to traveling interstate. He'd often come home to Melbourne a couple of times a week, but then was off again the next day, checking on his family's department stores all over the country. It kept him busy.

As did the women he dated.

Not that they gave him much satisfaction anymore. He pretended to enjoy their company and he even tried to enjoy a good-night kiss, but whenever he tried to take it further something held him back. He just didn't want any of these women.

He wanted only Jenna.

Damn her.

But what was the use of wanting someone who was a liar and a cheat? Someone who had tried to con him and his family out of money they had nothing to do with? Dammit, when he thought about Jenna approaching his parents about Liam...telling them their dead son owed money...he could feel his blood boil.

And he refused to think about her being pregnant. Okay, so that was something he couldn't lay blame on her for. The broken condom had been an unfortunate incident, that's all. Beyond that he couldn't think about it—*wouldn't* think about it. It just wasn't going to happen.

He was at the office the following week when his PA announced he had some visitors. He groaned to himself as Chelsea and Todd came into his office. He'd spoken to Todd a couple of days after Chelsea had run out of the restaurant all those weeks ago. Things were going well for them now and they were trying for another baby.

Since then, he'd returned Todd's calls a couple of times and acted as natural as possible, but he had heard the worry in his friend's voice. Todd had remembered it had been the anniversary of Maddie's death, besides realizing Adam wasn't seeing Jenna anymore. Adam hadn't elaborated on the latter.

"We were just walking by and decided to stop in and see you," Todd said, his eyes sharpening as he did a quick study of Adam. "So, how have you been?"

"Busy." Adam gave him a wry smile as he gestured for them to sit down.

"We've just had two weeks in Paris," Chelsea bubbled.

Something inside Adam relaxed as he sat down on his chair. Happiness had eluded him, but he'd never wish the same for his friends.

He smiled across the desk at her, his first genuine smile for Chelsea in many months. "You're looking very happy."

"I am," she said, reaching out and taking hold of Todd's

hand beside her. "It was so romantic. Todd really knows how to sweep a girl off her feet."

"She's as light as a feather," Todd quipped, winking at Adam, not looking the least embarrassed. He'd earned his right to romanticize his wife.

Then Todd's eyes narrowed. "Everything okay with you?"

"Sure." Adam appreciated his friend's concern, but he didn't really need it.

Just then, Todd's cell phone rang. He was instantly all business. "Excuse me. I have to answer this." He got up and was speaking into his phone as he went in the outer office.

Chelsea immediately sat forward on her chair, not smiling now. "This is awkward for me, Adam," she said, keeping her voice low. "But I want to apologize to you. I know I made you uncomfortable. I went a little crazy there. I lost the…baby…and it seemed like Todd didn't care."

Adam's heart constricted for her loss. "It's okay. I understand."

"Please don't tell Todd how I…harassed you. I really do only think of you as a friend."

It was a relief to hear her say that. "I won't."

She held his gaze, reading the sincerity in his eyes. Then she sat back on her chair. "Todd said you're not seeing Jenna anymore."

He could feel himself freeze up. "No, I'm not."

"I'm sorry. She seemed very nice."

"Yes, she did, didn't she?"

Thankfully, Todd came back and the conversation turned to more mundane things. They didn't stay long after that and left with his promise to visit them soon.

No sooner had they left, than his mother came marching into his office, parental purpose in her elegant steps. Adam swore under his breath. Was this some sort of conspiracy or what? So far he'd managed to avoid her these past two weeks.

"You haven't been returning my calls, Adam," Laura Roth said.

"I've been traveling around. Didn't Dad tell you?"

"Of course he told me. So did Dominic, but that doesn't make up for not hearing your voice myself."

"Mum, I've been busy."

"Yes, I know. I've seen the women you've been busy with in the papers."

He stiffened. "You have a problem with that?"

"What happened to Jenna? She was lovely."

How could he tell her anything close to the truth? Liam had been innocent of the crime, but why give his mother something more to think about in her grief? It was unnecessary that she know.

"It didn't work out. Sometimes that happens. Not everyone is compatible."

His mother shook her head. "No, you two were definitely compatible." She watched him steadily. "I think you're just scared after Maddie."

He felt the pain, then pushed it away. In any case, perhaps it was best she believe that. It would save any further hassle.

He shrugged. "I can't help what you think, Mum."

She held his gaze. "I really thought you might find happiness with Jenna."

"Did you?"

She made a face. "I can see you don't want to talk."

"No, I don't. I'm a busy man." Then gently, he said, "I'm sorry."

She didn't say anything for a moment. "So am I, Adam.

Sorry you're going to end up old and alone with no one to love you," she said, not appeased.

He raised an eyebrow at her. "So that means *you* won't love me when I'm old and alone?"

She gave him a light smack on the arm, then kissed him and left. His mother had said Jenna was a keeper the day they'd all lunched together at his parents' place. She'd been wrong about that. Laura Roth was the one to keep.

At least he could relax now that his mother had caught up with him. And maybe now she would rest easier knowing she couldn't do anything more. He prayed she'd leave it alone anyway. There was nothing anyone could do. He missed Jenna, but he would learn to live without her. He'd learned to live without Maddie, hadn't he? And Maddie had been the love of his life.

So the last person he expected to see coming out of a movie theatre in the city one evening was Jenna. He'd just been to a business dinner in a nearby restaurant, and was about to cross the road to where his driver was waiting in the car when he literally ran into her.

"Adam!" she exclaimed softly.

He reached out to steady her as something deep inside steadied, too. He wanted to hold on, not let her go, as if she was the balance he needed to subsist.

Then he remembered what she'd done.

He dropped his hands and broke free. "Hello, Jenna," he said, unable to quite tear his eyes completely away from her, despite the anger still smoldering inside his chest.

Then someone coughed.

It was the woman beside her.

Jenna seemed to recover. "This is my sister-in-law, Vicki."

Stewart's wife.

Curious, he inclined his head at the other woman, but

received a hostile nod instead. Clearly he was persona non grata to the Branson family. Not that he cared. He'd come up against less friendly people in the boardroom and won.

His eyes were drawn back to Jenna. "You look good," he said, and meant it.

She moistened her lips. "So do you."

Time took a pause.

In the streetlight he was suddenly aware that she'd lost weight. There was a hint of dark circles under her eyes, too. His chest lurched as he wondered if he was to blame, but as quickly he knew he wasn't. She and her brother had caused all this from the start. He wouldn't feel sorry for her.

And then something hit him. God help him, but if she'd lost weight then at least she shouldn't be pregnant. If she was, surely she'd be putting on weight by now? A powerhouse of relief washed through him. He could not have handled knowing he was to become a father again. It would have been the ultimate cruelty.

Vicki slipped her arm through Jenna's in a protective manner. "Come on," she said firmly. "We have to be going."

Jenna hesitated. "How's Todd? And Chelsea?"

He allowed that she did have some genuine concern for others. "They're doing okay. They worked it out."

Her face relaxed a little. "I'm glad."

"Yeah, me, too."

Vicki tightened her arm. "Jenna, let's go."

Jenna nodded. "Yes, we should."

The two women went to turn away.

"How's Stewart?" he found himself saying.

They both stopped.

"He's coming home in a couple of weeks." It was Vicki who spoke in a curt tone before she guided Jenna away.

He turned and crossed the street to where his driver waited in the car. There was nothing else to say. He doubted he'd ever see Jenna Branson again. And that was just as well.

Jenna didn't think she could have driven them back to Vicki's house, so she was grateful her sister-in-law insisted on doing the driving. She felt sick after seeing Adam.

Oh, God, he'd looked so gorgeous that her heart had ached for him. And it ached even more when she remembered all the women he'd been seen dating recently. The newspapers had even commented on how hard "the playboy had been playing lately."

"Come inside for a drink," Vicki said, bringing the car to a stop in the driveway of her house twenty minutes later.

Jenna pulled herself together. "Thanks, but no. I should be going home. I've got work tomorrow." It was a weeknight, but Vicki had insisted Jenna needed to get out and relax and that it couldn't wait until the weekend.

Vicki frowned. "Sweetie, I can see you're upset. Come inside for a little while." She put her hand up when Jenna opened her mouth to refuse. "No. I insist."

Jenna knew when to give up. "Okay."

Once they were inside the babysitter left to go home next door, then they checked that the girls were sleeping before she and Vicki headed to the living room.

"How about a glass of sherry?"

Jenna's stomach turned. "Do you have any mineral water?"

"Sure. Or I could make coffee or a hot chocolate. Or how about—"

Jenna felt nausea rise in her throat. "I'm sorry, I—" She

ran for the bathroom, where she was sick. She didn't realize Vicki was there until she finished throwing up.

"You're pregnant, aren't you?"

Twelve

"You son of a—!" a male voice growled down the telephone line.

"What do you want, Branson?" Adam cut in, scowling. When his PA had said Stewart Branson was on the line, he hadn't expected this. He'd only seen Jenna last night. What the hell were they up to now?

There was a low curse. "You couldn't help yourself, could you? You just had to have her."

Adam's hand tightened around the phone. He didn't discuss his sex life with anyone. "Look, I'm heading out of the office to catch a plane. Perhaps we can continue this fascinating conversation another time."

"Don't hang up or you'll regret it," the other man warned.

"I don't take kindly to threats."

"No, you just like to give them."

Adam's jaw tightened. "Branson, *I'm* not the one who tried to get money under false pretenses."

"It wasn't supposed to go so far. Jenna wasn't supposed to—"

"Scam me?" Adam scoffed. "Come on. I'm not the lowlife who left the country, then used his sister to do his dirty work."

There was an abrupt pause. "It wasn't like that."

"Frankly, I don't care what it was like. It's over, Branson." Another moment and he'd hang up. He wanted to get on with his life, not listen to this guy justifying actions that had been criminal in the first place.

"I admit I have a gambling problem," Branson said quickly, as if knowing the call was about to end. "And I'm going to rectify that when I get home. But leave Jenna out of it. She knew nothing. She thought she was helping me."

Something in his tone stopped Adam from putting the phone down there and then. "You're just trying to scam me again, Branson." The man was probably trying to get him back with Jenna…and an unending supply of Roth cash. And if not cash, then the Roth connections were certainly a drawcard. He wasn't falling for it.

"I wish to hell it *was* a scam," Stewart muttered.

Adam stiffened. "What does that mean?"

"What I did was wrong, Roth, but what you did in getting my sister pregnant and not taking responsibility is far worse."

Adam's breath stopped dead. "What did you say?" he croaked, not caring that he was showing the shock rolling through him. He felt as if someone had sliced his chest open.

"Jenna's pregnant. And I expect you to do something about it."

Adam shuddered, then inhaled some air and started to

breathe again. This couldn't be. Jenna had lost weight. She would have said.

Or would she?

"Roth? Did you hear me?"

Adam swallowed. "Leave it with me," he managed to say.

"So you'll go see Jenna and fix things?"

"Yes."

"Good." There was a pause. "No one else knows yet, Roth, except me and my wife. I'm giving you time to make things right." The other man disconnected the call.

Adam sat there and stared at the hand piece before slowly putting it down to rest. Usually, he would never let another man hang up on him or threaten him. It was a measure of his complete and utter shock. Yet he had to admire Stewart Branson for taking a stand for his sister.

Jenna.

She'd once told him she was his worst nightmare. Right now he had to agree. She was pregnant...having his baby... and he doubted Stewart Branson was going to like the outcome.

After seeing Adam last night, Jenna hadn't been able to face going to work today so she'd called in sick. And she *was* sick—with morning sickness. She'd started feeling off-color a few weeks ago, but this morning she'd been feeling light-headed and nauseous, the morning sickness seeming to hit her with all its force. It was as if now that she'd acknowledged it, its very strength had intensified.

She'd suspected she was pregnant after she'd missed her last period. She just hadn't wanted to take the test. But after she'd been ill last night at Vicki's place, her sister-in-law had taken that out of her hands and had gone out to the local pharmacy and bought a pregnancy kit. It had confirmed her worst fears.

She was pregnant.

But was it really her worst fear? For all the problems ahead of her, she wanted this child more than anything. How could she *not* want the child of the man she loved? With new wonder she touched her stomach again, aware of a life beating beneath her heart. It was the most glorious feeling on earth.

Of course it didn't discount the fact that she had some heavy-duty thinking to do. She'd made Vicki promise not to tell Adam. He wanted nothing to do with her and seeing him again last night had merely confirmed that. His eyes may have eaten her up for that initial moment when they'd run into each other, but they'd soon hardened again. He thought she was a dreadful person. He would not want her to have his child.

On the other hand, she couldn't quite let the feeling go that a man had a right to know he was going to be a father. She would be distressed to *not* tell Adam. It would feel dishonest, and if he found out the truth later wouldn't it confirm his low opinion of her?

Yet with all his wealth, he might even try to take her baby away from her and raise it himself. The thought made her feel more than physically ill. It made her feel heartsick. Could she really believe he'd do that? Could she afford to believe he *wouldn't?* And if that were the case, wouldn't it be stupid of her to tell him about the baby at all?

Oh, God, her head was spinning.

Right then her doorbell rang. She jumped. No one knew she'd stayed home today, except the people at work. She hoped to high heaven it wasn't Marco. She really couldn't stomach him right now and would probably be rude.

Hopefully, it was only Vicki. Her sister-in-law might

have called her at work and learned she'd stayed home, and had decided to check on her. The phone had rung a couple of times this morning, but she hadn't answered. And she'd turned off her cell phone, too. She hadn't wanted to see people today.

The doorbell rang again and this time the person kept their finger on it. Already she had a headache and the sound went right through her, making her head swim. She rushed to answer it. Vicki would be worried about her, but all the same—

"Adam!" Her knees turned weak when she saw who it was, and she had to grab the door handle to hold herself up.

He stepped past her into the apartment without any greeting whatsoever. This was obviously not going to be a friendly visit.

Heart thumping with dismay, she slowly closed the door and turned to face him. The last time he'd been here was over a month ago. He'd been angry and upset then. Looking at him now, she knew nothing had changed. He *still* looked angry and upset, a pulse beating in his jaw, his nostrils flaring. Outside the movie theatre last night may not have happened. Clearly, she'd been wrong that he might have been glad to see her, if only for a heartbeat.

And then something occurred to her. Could Vicki have told him? She instantly dismissed that. Her sister-in-law had promised she wouldn't. Vicki knew she needed time to think about this.

"Adam, why are—"

"I owe you an apology, Jenna." He cut right across her in a hard voice.

She blinked. It was the last thing she expected him to say. "You do?"

He stood there watching her, his whole body tense,

telling her something was terribly wrong in spite of the apology. "You weren't trying to scam me about the money for your brother. I know that now. I'm sorry I accused you of something you didn't do."

She frowned. The words coming out of his mouth didn't match the angry look of him. "How do you know all this?"

"Stewart told me the truth," he said curtly. "He phoned me."

She was trying to get her head around that. "Stewart?"

Her brother was going to get help for his addiction as soon as he came back to Australia, but where Adam was concerned Stewart had been more than pleased to let sleeping dogs lie. She swallowed, suddenly getting a bad feeling about this. If Stewart had told Adam the truth, then why was Adam still looking so furious? Surely he'd be relieved she'd been telling the truth.

She could feel a mounting sense of panic. "I don't understand. Why would he call you now? It's over and done with."

"He wanted to abuse the hell out of me."

"For you not believing me?"

"That—" a pulse ticked beneath the taut skin of one cheek "—and other things."

She swallowed hard. Dear God. "Oth-other things?"

He stood in the middle of the living room. "You should have told me, Jenna," he grated harshly. "You should have said something."

A shiver went through her. What was he talking about? Was this merely about—

"You should have told me about the baby."

In an instant the air was sucked from the room.

"You know?" she whispered, unable to move, unable to do anything but try and get through the next seconds.

He gave a hard jerk of his head. "I know," he rasped. "Your brother blasted me about you not more than half an hour ago."

"Oh, God." Her feet moved then, and she made her way to the couch, sinking onto it before she fell down in a heap. Adam knew she was carrying his child. He was here to see her about it. She wasn't prepared. She didn't know what she was going to do...or say to him. It was all so new to her.

She moistened her mouth and looked across at him. "Vicki promised she wouldn't tell you, but I didn't think about her telling anyone else." Another thought came to mind and she groaned. "Oh, God, he's probably telling my parents right now."

"No. He said only he and Vicki know at this stage." His lips twisted. "Your brother's giving me the chance to make things right."

That was something at least.

"You weren't going to tell me at all, were you?" he said icily, drawing her focus back to him.

"Um...I don't know. I only found out for sure last night." She explained about returning to Vicki's and becoming sick. As she finished speaking she suddenly noticed how white he was around the mouth.

Through anger?

Or angst?

"You're not pleased about the news." It wasn't a question. She could see it was a fact.

He stood there, not moving. "No, I'm not pleased."

In spite of everything, the words caught at her heartstrings and she hugged her stomach. "I won't get rid of my baby, Adam. Don't ask me to."

His face turned pale. "I didn't...I wouldn't."

Her shoulders sagged a little. There was no way she'd have an abortion, but she was glad to hear him say it.

"But this is the one time I can't do the right thing, Jenna," he said, his jaw tightening with absolute firmness. "I have strong feelings for you, but I can't marry you. And I can't be a father to the child."

She managed to lift her chin. "I don't think I've asked anything of you yet, Adam."

"I know, but I want to assure you I'll still set you and the child up for a life. I'll even acknowledge in writing that the child is mine. It's just that…" He swallowed. "I can't be involved with it at all."

Her nerves tightened. "That 'it' you refer to is your own flesh and blood," she choked, unable to let him get away with this one thing. This was *their* baby they were talking about.

His head reeled back, and he heaved in a breath then slowly expelled it. "Yes, you're right." He pushed a hand through his hair. "Look, I need to explain something. I don't want you thinking…" He stopped for a second, his eyes turning dark with inner pain. "My wife was pregnant when she died in the car accident."

Jenna gasped. "Oh, my God, Adam."

His eyes said he appreciated her sympathy. "We'd known for a few weeks, but we hadn't told the family. We were going to tell them that night at a dinner party."

She knew immediately. "The balloons. Your wife was bringing them home for the party, wasn't she?"

He nodded jerkily. "We didn't get to tell the family the news about the baby, and I didn't tell them afterward, either. Only Todd knows. I almost drank myself to death after that, but he came around and made me get up and start living again. He was relentless. He wouldn't let me be." He took a shuddering breath. "I owe him a bloody hell of a lot."

Now it made sense why Adam had been so determined not to encourage Todd's wife.

"Adam, I'm *so* sorry." She wanted to get up and go to him, but she sensed he couldn't handle her touching him right now. He was holding on to his control by mere threads. Her being pregnant had brought all this up again for him.

"I loved Maddie and I loved my unborn child," he said with full sincerity. "Losing them almost killed me. It *did* kill a part of me. I'm not capable of going through that pain again. I'm sorry, Jenna. I really am."

Jenna's heart broke for him. She could only imagine what it was like to lose his wife, his child, his whole world. If anything happened to him—to *their* child—she knew she wouldn't have a life without them. She'd merely exist.

As Adam existed.

In her heart of hearts she knew what she had to do. She'd let him pay for the upkeep of his child. She'd even let him pay for some of her own expenses, so that she could look after their child properly. But what she would never do now was tell him she loved him. She wouldn't burden him in such a way. It would only add too much guilt to a man who already felt far too much responsibility for his family and friends. A man who'd already been through so much…lost so much more.

Her eyes stung and she blinked the tears back as she pushed herself off the couch to stand up. "Adam, I—" Suddenly she felt dizzy. She stopped to get her balance, thinking she'd gotten up too quickly.

"Jenna, are you okay?"

"I—" She vaguely heard Adam's voice just before everything turned black.

"What the hell!" Adam watched Jenna begin to topple over. He lunged forward before she could fall to the floor, and she collapsed unconscious in his arms like a rag doll, her face white.

He felt the blood drain out of him. "Oh, my God," he said hoarsely, and stretched her out on the couch, putting a cushion under her head. Then he knelt beside her, tapping her face. "Jenna, wake up."

She just lay there.

His lungs were tight. He could barely breathe. He swallowed a lump of fear in his throat and tapped her face again. This time she began to come around. "Thank God," he murmured, falling back on his heels with relief.

But only for a moment. An instant later he surged upward and moved to sit beside her. "Jenna?"

She opened her eyes and blinked. "What happened?"

"You fainted."

Her forehead wrinkled. "Fainted?" She went to get up, then lay back down. "I feel so dizzy." She swallowed. "My ear is really sore now. I'm starting to feel nauseated again, too."

He shot to his feet. "Stay there. I'll get you a bucket or something, then I'm calling my doctor." He strode into the kitchen and found a small bucket under the kitchen sink. It would do. He took it back into the living room, along with a towel, and put both beside her on the floor.

She had her eyes closed and seemed to be resting. His hands shook as he flipped open his cell phone and called the family doctor. Oscar was in a consultation, but Adam insisted on speaking to him and the receptionist immediately put him through.

Adam told him the problem in a rush then ended with, "She's pregnant, Oscar."

A pause came down the line. "Is she hemorrhaging or having any other problems with the baby?" Oscar asked sharply.

Adam had already thought of that. "No, I don't think so. She's just dizzy."

"To be on the safe side, I'll call an ambulance anyway. Now give me the address. I'll meet you at the hospital."

Fear jumped inside Adam's chest, but he managed to tell the doctor the address.

"And Adam, it'll be fine. It's probably more to do with morning sickness than anything else."

"I hope you're right, Oscar." Adam hung up. He could hear the understanding in Oscar's voice. Apart from Todd, only the medical people at the hospital had known Maddie had been pregnant. Oscar had been one of them.

He crouched back down beside Jenna, his chest so tight watching her lie there with her eyes still closed. "Jenna?" he said gently, touching her arm. "The doctor's going to send around an ambulance."

She lifted her eyelids, fear flickering in her eyes.

"There's nothing to worry about. It's only a precaution. My doctor thinks it may just be some morning sickness."

Her hand went to her stomach in a protective fashion. "It's probably best."

Something twisted inside Adam as he sat on the floor next to her, not caring about his clothes, not caring about anything but Jenna right then. He wouldn't let himself think about the baby. This was about Jenna. He had to get her well again.

Time ticked by.

"Adam?"

"Yes?"

"I think I'm a little scared."

"Don't be." But his heart was thudding almost out of his chest. He felt so helpless. "Would you like a drink of water or something?"

"No." She swallowed. "Just you."

"I can supply that." He held her hand, realizing she felt

hot. She must have a temperature, too. Oh, God, that didn't sound like morning sickness to him.

"Adam, I'm sorry."

"For what?"

"For doing this to you. I'll be fine. I really will."

"I know you will. And there's *nothing* to be sorry for." He touched her cheek. "Now rest. They'll be here soon."

They were, but it wasn't soon enough for Adam's liking. He would have read them the riot act if he hadn't been so damn relieved to see them.

The paramedic seemed to think the baby was fine, but Adam didn't relax until the doctors at the hospital had thoroughly checked her over and diagnosed an ear infection. Then they gave her some antibiotics that were safe for early pregnancy to stop any further infection, and something for the dizziness that had a mild sedative effect, and said they were keeping her in overnight. He felt much better about it all once Jenna was tucked up in bed in the private room he'd insisted they give her. He would pay. He didn't care about the money.

"I think I should call your parents," he suggested, as she was nodding off.

Her eyes burst open. "Don't let them find out about the baby."

He squeezed her hand. "I'll make sure no one tells them."

She sighed and closed her eyes. "Thank you," she murmured, then her eyelids fluttered open briefly. "Vicki might tell them. Don't let her," she ended as she fell asleep.

The thought of calling her parents wasn't pleasant, but the thought of calling Jenna's sister-in-law gave him an on-the-spot headache. The woman had despised him last night. Still, he had to speak to her first so that she wouldn't inadvertently mention the baby.

Thankfully he'd had the forethought to grab Jenna's keys, handbag and cell phone from the side table as they'd left her apartment. No doubt her parents' telephone number and Vicki's would be on speed dial.

Jenna's sister-in-law was upset, then cold with him, but he got an assurance she would say nothing about the baby. "For Jenna's sake, not yours," she snapped. She suggested that she call her in-laws, but Adam felt he should do it himself. She hung up after saying she'd be there soon.

Then he called the Bransons, who were alarmed, naturally, but he assured them Jenna was fine.

After that, he sat by the bed and waited.

They all arrived half an hour later, and once they saw for themselves that Jenna was okay, they turned their attention more fully on him. Vicki couldn't quite hide her hostility, but Jenna's parents seemed very nice and were grateful he had been there for their daughter. No doubt her parents thought Vicki's attitude was because of Stewart. They, at least, didn't appear to hold their son's addiction problems against him.

But all of them had a question in their eyes that he couldn't answer. He knew they were wondering why he'd been with Jenna today. It was obvious her parents knew about their previous relationship. No doubt he'd be considered the worst kind of person once they learned of the baby, especially once they knew he wouldn't marry their daughter. Hell, he felt disgusted in himself, too. He couldn't blame them.

"I have to go pick up the children," Vicki said, looking at her watch half an hour later.

"Yes, you go do that, love," Joyce Branson said. "We'll stay with Jenna until she wakes up."

"There's no need for you to stay," Adam said firmly, and

received a speculative look from the others. "I'm happy to call you when Jenna wakes up."

"Thank you, Adam," Joyce said, "but I wouldn't feel right leaving my daughter."

Adam glanced away before they could see his irritation. He wanted to be with Jenna by himself. Time was running out for him. He and Jenna didn't have much longer to be together.

"Of course…" Tony Branson said, drawing Adam's eyes to Jenna's father, "Joyce and I could really do with a cup of coffee. I'm sure there must be a cafeteria around here somewhere."

Adam nodded at him. He knew what the other man was doing and he was grateful.

Once they left, Adam felt the tension ease inside him. Jenna was still sleeping, and he was happy to sit by her side for now. Just him and Jenna together.

But as he sat there, as the minutes ticked by, it began to sink in that it wasn't fair to Jenna for him to stay too long. He'd have to leave eventually.

For good.

At the thought, he dropped his head into his hands, everything weighing heavily on his mind. At least he knew Jenna's family would help look after her and the baby. They were decent people. He would provide what he could with monetary assistance, but that's all he could offer her. She and the baby deserved better than a man who'd lost a large chunk of his heart five years ago.

Taking a shuddering breath, he lifted his head. God, how could he have been so wrong about her? She looked so peaceful lying there, so beautiful. She was a person who touched other people. A person who touched *him*.

And then it hit him.

He loved her.

Like an exorcism, his inner demons left him in that instant, taking his grief with them, repairing the hole in his heart and filling it with a new, stronger love.

He loved Jenna.

He loved their baby.

He couldn't let either of them go.

Thirteen

Jenna opened her eyes to a dimly lit room. She blinked as she tried to adjust to where she was, then she saw Adam sitting in the chair beside the bed and everything came rushing back. She was in hospital!

"The baby?" she whispered, her heart filling her throat.

Adam was on his feet instantly. "It's okay. Our baby is fine."

She sighed with relief. Then she realized something. Had he said "our" baby? Maybe she was hearing things because of the ear infection?

"How are you feeling now?" he asked.

She lifted her head and tried to sit up. "I'm not as dizzy anymore."

"The medication must be working." He gave her a gentle smile as he helped her get more comfortable against the pillows. "You'll be better in next to no time."

There was something different about him, but she couldn't quite pinpoint it. Then she remembered, and panic rose inside her. "My parents? And Vicki? Did they come? Are they here? Did Vicki tell them about the baby?"

His smile warmed even more. "Yes, they were here. And no, they still don't know about the baby. That's up to you to tell them when you're ready."

Her shoulders slumped with relief. At least she didn't have to face them over that just yet. "That's good, then."

He nodded. "I convinced them to go home for a few hours. I said I'd call them once you woke up."

"Thank you." Then she bit her lip. "You didn't have to stay with me, Adam."

"Yes, my love, I did." He placed his lips on her forehead. "I want to stay with you the rest of my life."

"Wh-what?"

He eased back and looked into her eyes. "I love you, Jenna. I'm not letting you go. Not now. Not ever."

"But—" She tried to get her head around what he was saying. "What about Maddie and the baby?"

He didn't flinch at all. "Maddie's at peace and so is our child. And for the first time since their deaths, I'm truly at peace, too." He kissed her hand. "I have no doubt I would have had a good life with Maddie, but it wasn't to be. You and I were meant to be together, darling."

She looked at him and her heart dared to hope. "Are you really sure?"

"I've never been more certain of anything in my life. Maddie was the love of my youth, Jenna, but *you* are the love of my *life*."

She thrilled to the words. "Oh, Adam."

"And you love me, too, don't you?"

"I'm that obvious?"

He leaned down to gently seal a kiss on her lips. "Love recognizes love, my darling. Will you marry me?"

"Yes!"

"Good. Your mother is already planning our wedding." He smiled as she blinked in surprise. "I had to get your parents out of here somehow. Otherwise I'd never have gotten you alone."

"So they're happy about it?"

"Definitely. And I'm sure they'll be even happier when they learn about the baby."

Jenna's heart rose with sheer happiness. Everything was falling into place now.

Adam was right. It was meant to be.

Epilogue

Babies abounded everywhere at Christmas later that year. Cassandra and Dominic had welcomed their second daughter, Eli, a month previously in November. Chelsea had joyously given birth to a baby boy only a week ago, making Todd a very happy father. And even Vicki and Stewart were expecting their third child in a couple of months' time.

For Jenna and Adam, their son, Christian Liam Roth, was born on Christmas Eve. They decided to name him "Christian" to celebrate their Christmas baby, and "Liam" in honor of the uncle he would never know, but who had brought his parents together. Laura and Michael Roth were the proudest of grandparents, as were Joyce and Tony Branson.

Jenna was allowed to come home from the hospital on Christmas Day, on the condition that she only go to the Roth family lunch if she took things easy. It had been Adam's one condition. He'd even arranged for her family to be at the lunch too, not that the Roths had minded sharing on this occasion. Considering that Adam had barely left her side the whole pregnancy and would make sure she didn't lift a finger today, she found his concern both amusing and touching.

She watched him check their sleeping son again in the bassinet, and she smiled with love. "You can relax now, darling."

He grinned ruefully. "I'll try."

As a new mum, she felt nervous herself, but this was more than that. She knew he'd never fully be able to relax and not worry about them. And she understood. She felt the same. She could only imagine what it would be like for him to let himself love so much when he knew the pain of loss so well.

Looking at their son now…looking at her husband…she wasn't so sure she would be quite as brave to love again. She thanked God that Adam had been able to open his heart. He loved her and Christian with an intensity that took her breath away.

"Did I tell you that you're my idol, Mr. Roth?"

He smiled adoringly at her. "I seem to remember you called me something entirely different when you were giving birth to our son yesterday."

She chuckled. "Don't let that fool you. I'm usually a very polite person."

He gave her a soft kiss. "Sweetheart, you fooled me the moment I met you. I didn't see you coming at all."

Jenna looked into Adam's eyes, her happiness true and complete. Love had found a way to heal all wounds, and now they could fully focus on the future.

And that looked very bright indeed.

* * * * *

COMING NEXT MONTH

Available December 7, 2010

REQUEST YOUR FREE BOOKS!

2 FREE NOVELS
PLUS 2
FREE GIFTS!

Passionate, Powerful, Provocative!

YES! Please send me 2 FREE Silhouette Desire® novels and my 2 FREE gifts (gifts are worth about $10). After receiving them, if I don't wish to receive any more books, I can return the shipping statement marked "cancel." If I don't cancel, I will receive 6 brand-new novels every month and be billed just $4.05 per book in the U.S. or $4.74 per book in Canada. That's a saving of at least 15% off the cover price! It's quite a bargain! Shipping and handling is just 50¢ per book.* I understand that accepting the 2 free books and gifts places me under no obligation to buy anything. I can always return a shipment and cancel at any time. Even if I never buy another book, the two free books and gifts are mine to keep forever.

225/326 SDN E5QG

Name	(PLEASE PRINT)

Address	Apt. #

City	State/Prov.	Zip/Postal Code

Signature (if under 18, a parent or guardian must sign)

Mail to the **Silhouette Reader Service:**
IN U.S.A.: P.O. Box 1867, Buffalo, NY 14240-1867
IN CANADA: P.O. Box 609, Fort Erie, Ontario L2A 5X3

Not valid for current subscribers to Silhouette Desire books.

Want to try two free books from another line?
Call 1-800-873-8635 or visit www.morefreebooks.com.

* Terms and prices subject to change without notice. Prices do not include applicable taxes. N.Y. residents add applicable sales tax. Canadian residents will be charged applicable provincial taxes and GST. Offer not valid in Quebec. This offer is limited to one order per household. All orders subject to approval. Credit or debit balances in a customer's account(s) may be offset by any other outstanding balance owed by or to the customer. Please allow 4 to 6 weeks for delivery. Offer available while quantities last.

Your Privacy: Silhouette Books is committed to protecting your privacy. Our Privacy Policy is available online at www.eHarlequin.com or upon request from the Reader Service. From time to time we make our lists of customers available to reputable third parties who may have a product or service of interest to you. If you would prefer we not share your name and address, please check here. ☐

Help us get it right—We strive for accurate, respectful and relevant communications. To clarify or modify your communication preferences, visit us at www.ReaderService.com/consumerschoice.

*See below for a sneak peek from our classic
Harlequin® Romance® line.*

Introducing DADDY BY CHRISTMAS by Patricia Thayer.

MIA caught sight of Jarrett when he walked into the open lobby. It was hard not to notice the man. In a charcoal business suit with a crisp white shirt and striped tie covered by a dark trench coat, he looked more Wall Street than small-town Colorado.

Mia couldn't blame him for keeping his distance. He was probably tired of taking care of her.

Besides, why would a man like Jarrett McKane be interested in her? Why would he want to take on a woman expecting a baby? Yet he'd done so many things for her. He'd been there when she'd needed him most. How could she not care about a man like that?

Heart pounding in her ears, she walked up behind him. Jarrett turned to face her. "Did you get enough sleep last night?"

"Yes, thanks to you," she said, wondering if he'd thought about their kiss. Her gaze went to his mouth, then she quickly glanced away. "And thank you for not bringing up my meltdown."

Jarrett couldn't stop looking at Mia. Blue was definitely her color, bringing out the richness of her eyes.

"What meltdown?" he said, trying hard to focus on what she was saying. "You were just exhausted from lack of sleep and worried about your baby."

He couldn't help remembering how, during the night, he'd kept going in to watch her sleep. How strange was that? "I hope you got enough rest."

She nodded. "Plenty. And you're a good neighbor for

coming to my rescue."

He tensed. Neighbor? *What neighbor kisses you like I did?* "That's me, just the full-service landlord," he said, trying to keep the sarcasm out of his voice. He started to leave, but she put her hand on his arm.

"Jarrett, what I meant was you went beyond helping me." Her eyes searched his face. "I've asked far too much of you."

"Did you hear me complain?"

She shook her head. "You should. I feel like I've taken advantage."

"Like I said, I haven't minded."

"And I'm grateful for everything…"

Grasping her hand on his arm, Jarrett leaned forward. The memory of last night's kiss had him aching for another. "I didn't do it for your gratitude, Mia."

Gorgeous tycoon Jarrett McKane has never believed in Christmas—but he can't help being drawn to soon-to-be-mom Mia Saunders! Christmases past were spent alone…and now Jarrett may just have a fairy-tale ending for all his Christmases future!

Available December 2010, only from Harlequin® Romance®.